Andrew listened t...

While he went to the othe... ..., Rachel gathered up the cards they were playing with his daughter. "Maybe we should play Candy Land next time," he heard her say to Maura. "I'm pretty good at that game."

"You really like Candy Land?" the girl asked.

"It was one of my favorite games when I was a kid."

"I didn't know it was that old," Maura said so solemnly that Rachel had to laugh.

"Even my mother played it when she was a little girl," she told the child.

"My mommy's dead," Maura told her.

"I know. I'm sorry."

"Maybe someday I could get a new mommy. But she'll have to be someone my daddy likes."

"That would probably help," Rachel agreed.

"Daddy likes you," Maura said.

And that was Andrew's cue. He stepped back into the room before his daughter proposed right there and then.

* * *

Those Engaging Garretts!: The Carolina Cousins

Dear Reader,

Last year, I wrote a miniseries called Those Engaging Garretts! The heroes of these stories were brothers who lived in the fictional town of Pinehurst, New York, and through the writing, I fell in love with Matthew, Jackson and Lukas.

When their stories were done, I didn't want to say goodbye to these characters. I wanted to write more stories about the Garretts—and thankfully my editors were willing to let me! Except that there were only three brothers, and they'd each found their happy ending....

So I shifted my attention southeast of Pinehurst and discovered Charisma, North Carolina, and The Carolina Cousins. I'm thrilled to introduce these new Garretts to you—beginning with siblings Andrew, Daniel and Nathan.

First up is sexy single dad Andrew, who is too busy raising his seven-year-old daughter to even think about romance. But when he walks into a local flower shop and meets Rachel Ellis, love unexpectedly begins to bloom....

I hope you enjoy *The Single Dad's Second Chance,* and, as you read this story, maybe you'll catch a glimpse of the special woman who just might steal Daniel's heart in *A Wife for One Year* (coming in August 2014).

Happy reading,

Brenda Harlen

The Single Dad's Second Chance

Brenda Harlen

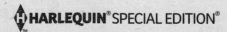

HARLEQUIN® SPECIAL EDITION®

Recycling programs
for this product may
not exist in your area.

ISBN-13: 978-0-373-65819-0

THE SINGLE DAD'S SECOND CHANCE

Copyright © 2014 by Brenda Harlen

Printed in U.S.A.

Books by Brenda Harlen

Harlequin Special Edition

**Prince Daddy & the Nanny #2147
**Royal Holiday Bride #2160
^The Maverick's
   Ready-Made Family #2215
¶From Neighbors...
   to Newlyweds? #2235
¶His Long-Lost Family #2278
¶A Very Special Delivery #2283
+A Maverick under the Mistletoe #2293
¶The Single Dad's Second Chance #2337

Silhouette Special Edition

*Her Best-Kept Secret #1756
The Marriage Solution #1811
∞One Man's Family #1827
The New Girl in Town #1859
**The Prince's Royal Dilemma #1898
**The Prince's Cowgirl Bride #1920
¤Family in Progress #1928
**The Prince's Holiday Baby #1942
§The Texas Tycoon's
   Christmas Baby #2016
ΔThe Engagement Project #2021
ΔThe Pregnancy Plan #2038
ΔThe Baby Surprise #2056
ΩThunder Canyon Homecoming #2079
**The Prince's Second Chance #2100

Harlequin Romantic Suspense

McIver's Mission #1224
Some Kind of Hero #1246
Extreme Measures #1282
Bulletproof Hearts #1313
Dangerous Passions #1394

*Family Business
∞Logan's Legacy Revisited
**Reigning Men
¤Back in Business
§The Foleys and the McCords
ΔBrides & Babies
ΩMontana Mavericks:
   Thunder Canyon Cowboys
^Montana Mavericks:
   Back in the Saddle
¶Those Engaging Garretts!
+Montana Mavericks:
   Rust Creek Cowboys

Other books by Brenda Harlen
available in ebook format.

BRENDA HARLEN

is a former family law attorney turned work-at-home mom and national bestselling author who has written more than twenty books for Harlequin. Her work has been validated by industry awards (including an RWA Golden Heart® Award and the *RT Book Reviews* Reviewers' Choice Award) and by the fact that her kids think it's cool that she's "a real author."

Brenda lives in southern Ontario with her husband and two sons. When she isn't at the computer working on her next book, she can probably be found at the arena, watching a hockey game. Keep up-to-date with Brenda on Facebook, follow her on Twitter, at @BrendaHarlen, or send her an email at brendaharlen@yahoo.com.

To all of the readers who asked for more "Garretts"—
thanks for welcoming my characters
into your lives and your hearts.

Chapter One

Rachel Ellis hated Valentine's Day.

Not that she'd ever admit as much to any of the customers who had formed an almost-steady stream of traffic through the door of Buds & Blooms since about 11:00 a.m., but she had expressed the sentiment—more than a few times already today—to her best friend and business partner, Holly Kendrick.

"Can you tell me," Rachel asked, when she went to the back during a rare quiet moment in the shop, "why so many men seem surprised to realize it's Valentine's Day when it falls on February 14 every single year?"

"Because they're men," Holly said simply.

"And is that why they also wait until the absolute last minute to buy flowers for their wives or girlfriends?"

"Yep."

"Next year we should offer discounts for advance orders." They had taken some, but those represented a small percentage of the sales already processed that day.

"It won't matter," Holly told her.

Rachel knew her friend was probably right. She sank down into a chair by the worktable. "I'm just going to take ten minutes to rest my feet before the next rush."

She only managed about half of that before the bell rang, indicating another customer had entered the shop.

Trish, a local college student who helped out part-time, showed up at two o'clock so that Holly could go home to get ready for her date with Shane—her on-again, off-again boyfriend of the past two years. Rachel, who had no plans, would stay until closing time at six o'clock.

It was quarter to the hour now, and there were only a couple of customers left in the shop. Her cheeks hurt from the smile she'd kept firmly plastered on her face as she boxed or wrapped order after order throughout the afternoon, and she was looking forward to the day being over.

But when Andrew Garrett walked through the door, just a few minutes before closing time, she didn't have to force the smile. He was a regular if not frequent customer, coming into Buds & Blooms three times a year without fail—Valentine's Day, August 10 and November 22. She didn't really know him. In fact, she only knew his name because it was on the credit card that he used to pay for his purchases. But for some inexplicable reason, her heart always beat just a little bit faster when he was around.

Or maybe it wasn't so inexplicable. After all, the man was a certified hunk. He stood about six-three with broad shoulders, narrow hips and long legs. His dark hair was neatly trimmed, and moss-green eyes looked out beneath straight brows. His jaw was cleanly shaven, his mouth was deliciously shaped, and when he'd smiled at her the first day he came into the shop, her knees had actually gone weak.

Then she'd dropped her gaze and noticed the well-worn gold band that circled the third finger of his left hand.

She should have expected as much—the only time gorgeous single men ever walked through the door of Buds & Blooms was Mother's Day.

February 14 had fallen on a Sunday that year, and he'd been one of the first customers through the door. He'd wanted a dozen white roses, and she'd laid the creamy white flowers out on top of a fan of ferns, added some baby's breath, then wrapped the arrangement in silver paper and clear cellophane and tied it together with white raffia. Even after three years, she remembered those details, and she wondered if that was evidence of the customer service she prided herself on or proof that she was pathetically infatuated with a handsome—and married—stranger.

"A dozen white roses?" she asked.

He smiled, and her heart did a funny little turn in her chest. "Good memory."

She went to the back to retrieve the flowers, then added the accent foliage and wrapped the arrangement. "Can I get you anything else today?"

He shook his head. "No, that's all."

She rang up the purchase and reached for the credit card he held out to her. Their fingers touched—briefly— in the transfer, but she felt a jolt at the unexpected contact.

Married, she reminded herself sternly.

And even if he wasn't, she'd made too many mistakes where the male gender was concerned to want to risk another one.

She processed the transaction and returned his card along with a receipt and his flowers.

"Thank you."

"You're welcome. And Happy Valentine's Day."

She kept the smile on her face until he'd walked out the door, then flipped the lock and wondered, *Why are the good ones always taken?*

* * *

As a single woman, Rachel really did hate Valentine's Day. But as a business owner counting the receipts, she had to love it. They'd sold more flowers in just ten hours today than they would in the rest of the month, and while Trish cleaned up the work counters in the back, Rachel restocked the display cases at the front of the store and made notes on what she would have to add to her orders this week.

"Do you want to go somewhere to grab a bite?" she asked Trish. Because of the thick gloves she wore in deference to the frigid temperature, she fumbled a little with the key as she locked up.

"Oh, um, that sounds great, but—"

"But you've got a date," Rachel guessed.

Her employee nodded.

"You should have said something—I could have finished up by myself."

"Doug had to work until eight tonight, anyway."

"Doug? The advertising guy?"

"Marketing," Trish clarified.

"I thought you dumped him."

"I did." She shrugged. "And then I missed him."

Rachel didn't know Doug, aside from what Trish had told her, so she bit her tongue. She wasn't so far past twenty that she didn't remember how it felt to be young and in love—or at least want to believe that she was. It had taken her a while, but she'd finally realized that being lonely in a relationship was worse than being alone.

She hadn't given up on the idea of finding someone to share her life with, but she'd stopped looking for her elusive soul mate around every corner.

"But I'll be in at seven tomorrow to help with the deliveries," Trish said now.

"I can handle the deliveries—if you can be here by ten, that's soon enough."

"Really?" The young woman looked as if Rachel had given her the moon instead of just three extra hours.

"Really," she confirmed.

"Thank you, thank you, thank you!"

Rachel couldn't help but smile at her exuberance. "Have a good time tonight."

"We will," Trish assured her.

Rachel waited until her employee got into her car and waved as she drove off. Because she lived only a couple of blocks from the shop, she walked to and from work. And usually she enjoyed the walk, but tonight, she was tired and hungry and just wanted to be home so she could snuggle on the couch with a bowl of popcorn to watch *Criminal Minds*.

Except that the way her stomach was growling, she knew popcorn was not going to suffice. When she got home, she exchanged her skirt and blouse for a favorite pair of jeans and a winter-white V-neck sweater, then slipped her feet into low-heeled boots and shrugged back into her coat. She burrowed her chin deeper into the collar when she stepped outside again and tried to ignore the cold as she headed toward Valentino's. Thankfully, the restaurant offered takeout because, even if she wanted to sit down and eat, she knew there was no way she'd get a table tonight.

Pulling open the door, she was immediately greeted by the mouthwatering scents of tomato, garlic and basil. Her stomach growled again. The woman behind the counter looked up and smiled. "Rachel, hi. Just let me put this order in to the kitchen and I'll tell Gemma that you're here."

"Don't…" Her protest trailed off as Maria had already disappeared into the kitchen.

Two minutes later, Gemma Palermo came through from the dining room.

"Happy Valentine's Day, *bella*." She kissed both of Rachel's cheeks, then looked past her friend and frowned. "You are alone?"

"I usually am," Rachel reminded her.

"But it's Valentine's Day," her friend said again.

"I know. And I didn't mean to take you away from your customers. I just wanted to get some pasta to take home—"

"Where you can eat alone?"

Rachel couldn't help but smile at the distress in Gemma's tone. "It's not illegal, you know."

"Maybe it should be."

But eating alone was Rachel's status quo, and she liked it that way. She was a smart, successful woman. She didn't need a man to make her life complete. She firmly and honestly believed that—most of the time. But she couldn't deny that the prospect of sitting alone in her empty condo eating penne with sausage and peppers from a plastic takeout container on Valentine's Day made her feel just a little bit pathetic.

"I've been on my feet all day," Rachel told her friend. "I just want—"

"To sit down," Gemma interrupted again. "Yes, you should sit down and have a nice glass of wine."

She nodded. "Actually, a glass of wine would be nice."

"Long day?"

"The longest."

Her friend nodded her understanding. "Tony refused to book any reservations past nine o'clock—otherwise, we'd be here all night."

"I guess you don't get to go out for dinner on Valentine's Day, either."

Her friend blushed. "We celebrated earlier. He made me breakfast in bed, and then... Well, let's just say we were almost late for work."

"Good thing he's the boss," Rachel noted.

"Only at the restaurant," Gemma said.

Rachel had to laugh. She'd gone to high school with both Gemma Battaglia and Tony Palermo. Tony's grandparents—Salvatore and Caterina Valentino—were the original owners of the restaurant when it first opened its doors almost fifty years earlier. It was, and continued to be, a family restaurant.

Tony had started bussing tables and washing dishes when he was ten years old, then he'd moved up to serving customers and helping with kitchen prep. Now he was the proprietor and head chef. Gemma had worked as a waitress in high school and for several years after, then she became a hostess and was now married to Tony. And so blissfully happy that she wanted all of her friends to be the same.

"Marco is working the bar tonight," Gemma said, referring to her youngest brother-in-law. "You tell him what you want to drink while I put your order in. Penne with sausage and peppers?"

She nodded, and her friend hurried off.

Rachel took a seat at the bar and requested a glass of valpolicella. She unbuttoned her coat as Marco poured the wine and set the glass on a napkin in front of her.

"How did you get stuck working Valentine's Day?" she asked.

"I volunteered," Marco admitted.

She raised her brows. "No plans with Tammy?"

"We broke up."

"I'm sorry."

He shrugged. "How about you? Why are you here instead of dancing the night away—and maybe getting lucky—with a handsome man who's not nearly good enough for you?"

"I'll consider it lucky if my feet will take me home again."

"If they won't—" he lifted her hand, touched his lips to the back of it "—I will."

She smiled at the twenty-two-year-old. "You better be careful, Marco, or one of these days, I just might take you up on that offer."

"I keep hoping."

Rachel knew him too well to take him seriously, but she couldn't deny that his casual flirtation was a nice boost to her ego.

"I should be out of here by ten," he said now. "We could go back to my place and—"

"Stop flirting with my friend," Gemma, back from the kitchen, chastised her brother-in-law.

His gaze didn't shift away from Rachel. "Why?"

"Because she'll break your heart."

"She does every single time I see her."

Gemma shook her head at him and said to Rachel, "I've got some counter space for you in the kitchen."

"It would be easier if you just let me take it home."

"It will taste better if you're among friends," Gemma insisted.

Rachel took the second glass of wine Marco poured for her and followed the hostess to the kitchen.

A stool was waiting at the end of a stainless steel workstation that was covered with a linen cloth and set up to replicate the tables in the dining room, complete with a lit candle inside a hurricane shade.

"Okay, this is better than eating out of a take-out container," Rachel admitted.

"Of course it is," Gemma agreed, as the pantry chef set a plate of salad and a small basket of artisan breads in front of Rachel. "I need to check on the dining room, but I'll be back in a few minutes."

As the kitchen staff continued with their rhythms and routines, Rachel dug into her salad. She was about halfway through the appetizer when Gemma returned to the kitchen.

"We can squeeze another chair in here," she was saying. "I'm sure Rachel would enjoy having some company."

"I appreciate the offer, but—"

"Then you won't insult me by turning it down," Gemma said.

The male voice sounded somewhat familiar, but Rachel couldn't place it—until she lowered her fork and looked up, into Andrew Garrett's green eyes.

Andrew appreciated that Gemma had the best of intentions and a good heart, but he really just wanted to take some pasta home and be alone. Or so he thought until he saw the pretty brunette from the flower shop seated at a makeshift table in the kitchen.

When she glanced up, the widening of her deep blue eyes reflected a surprise that mirrored his own. "Oh, um, hi."

He smiled. "Hi, yourself."

The hostess's gaze shifted from one to the other. "You know each other?"

"Sort of," he said.

At the same time the florist responded, "Not really."

"Well, that clears everything up," Gemma said drily.

"Mr. Garrett's been in to Buds & Blooms a few times," she explained.

"Andrew," he told her, and, realizing that they'd never been formally introduced, offered his hand.

"Rachel Ellis," she replied.

"Why are you eating in the kitchen?" he asked her.

"Because no one wants to be alone on Valentine's Day," the hostess answered.

Rachel's cheeks flushed. "Because Gemma refused to let me take my food home."

"There seems to be a lot of that going around," Andrew noted.

"We have a couple paying their bill and no one waiting for their table, if you wanted to move into the dining room," Gemma suggested.

Rachel shook her head, immediately and vehemently. "I'm good here."

His instinctive response was the same. If they dined together in the kitchen, they could share pasta and casual conversation. But if they ate in the dining room, with soft lighting and romantic music, it would take on a whole different ambience—almost like a date.

"Looks like a pretty good setup," he said to Rachel. "Do you mind if I join you?"

"Of course not," she said.

The words were barely out of her mouth before a waiter was at the table, setting another place. One of the chefs immediately put a salad on the table for him.

"I almost think there's better service here than in the dining room," he teased Gemma.

"Now I'm thinking that I should put your pasta in a take-out container and send you home," she countered.

He was tempted to say "please," but given a choice between sharing a meal with the florist and eating alone, he had to go with the florist.

"The truth is," he said instead, "the culinary genius of the chef is second only to the beauty of the restaurant's hostess."

Gemma laughed. "Flattery will get you anywhere you want to go in my restaurant, but now I must go back to work."

When she'd exited the kitchen, Andrew picked up his fork and stabbed a piece of lettuce. He and Rachel ate in silence for a few minutes, and though his dinner companion said nothing, he could imagine the questions that were running through her mind.

"I'm impressed," he said, when he'd finished his appetizer.

She sipped her wine. "By the salad?"

"By your restraint."

She didn't pretend to misunderstand. "It's not any of my business."

"But you're wondering why I'm not having dinner with the woman I bought the flowers for," he guessed.

"The thought did cross my mind."

"The flowers were for my wife," he told her. "But she died three years ago."

"I'm sorry," she said sincerely. "How long were you married?"

"Five years."

One of the kitchen assistants cleared away their salad plates and another immediately set bowls of steaming pasta on the table. He looked from his to hers, noticed they were the same.

Rachel speared a chunk of spicy sausage with her fork, popped it into her mouth.

"What about you?" he asked. "Why are you alone tonight?"

"I'm on a dating hiatus," she admitted.

"Why?"

She shrugged. "I made a lot of bad choices with respect to relationships, so I decided to take a break from men."

"How long have you been on this break?" he wondered.

"Sixteen months."

"You haven't been on a date in more than a year?"

"No," she admitted. "But even when I was dating, I never liked dating on Valentine's Day."

"Why not?"

"There's too much pressure to make a simple date into something more on February 14, too many expectations on both parties." She nibbled on her penne. "Did you know that ten percent of all marriage proposals take place on Valentine's Day?"

He shook his head.

"It makes me wonder—is the popularity of proposals on that day a result of romance in the air or a consequence of the pressure to celebrate in a big way?"

"The Valentine's Day chicken and egg," he mused.

She nodded. "And then there are the Valentine's Day weddings, which seem to me the lazy man's way of ensuring he'll remember his anniversary."

Andrew waited a beat before he said, "Nina and I were married on Valentine's Day."

Chapter Two

Rachel pushed her plate aside as her cheeks filled with color. "I don't think I can finish this with my foot in my mouth."

Andrew smiled and nudged her plate back to her. "We were actually married the twenty-second of November."

"Since I tend to speak without thinking, I'll forgive you for that," she said, picking up her fork again.

Gemma bustled into the kitchen, her eyes sparkling and her cheeks flushed with excitement. "Look at this," she said, holding her hand out to show off the princess-cut diamond solitaire on the tip of her finger. "Isn't it stunning?"

"It's beautiful," Rachel agreed. "But you're already married."

The hostess rolled her eyes. "It's not for me, obviously. One of our customers is going to propose to his girlfriend, right here, tonight.

"He told me the story when he called to make the reservation. They met on a blind date in our dining room, and he said the minute he first saw her, he knew she was the one. Now, eight months later, he's ready to ask her to share his life."

"So why do you have the ring?" Rachel wondered.

"Oh. Right." She turned to call out to the pastry chef. "Edouard—I need a tiramisu." Then she continued her explanation: "That's what she had for dessert that first night."

"You're not going to bury the ring in the cake, are you?" Andrew asked.

"No, I'm going to put it on top," Gemma explained. "The dark chocolate will really make the gold shine and the diamond sparkle."

"And the band sticky so she can't get it off her finger if she changes her mind," Rachel mused.

He grinned; the hostess scowled.

"You don't appreciate romance," she scolded Rachel.

"I do appreciate romance," his dinner companion insisted. "I've even done bouquets with engagement rings tied to the ribbon. But I think that words spoken from the heart make a more memorable proposal than the staged presentation of a ring."

"What about a 'will you marry me?' spelled out on the big screen at a sporting event?" Andrew asked.

Rachel opened her mouth to respond, then snapped it shut again and eyed him warily. "Is that how you proposed?"

He chuckled. "No."

"Should we make a wager on what her response will be?" Andrew asked, as Gemma left the kitchen with the dessert.

Rachel shook her head. "I might not be a fan of public proposals, but I hope she accepts. He obviously put a lot of thought into his plans tonight, bringing her back to the restaurant where they first met, remembering the dessert she had on that first date.

"And I don't think he'd pop the question in this kind of venue if he wasn't sure of the answer," she noted, before asking him, "How did you propose?"

"Oh." He pushed his now-empty bowl aside. "It wasn't very well planned out at all."

Her lips curved, making him suspect that the tips of his ears had gone red as they sometimes did when he was embarrassed.

"Impulsive…and in bed," she guessed.

Since he couldn't deny it, he only said, "She said yes."

Her smile widened, and he couldn't help noticing the way it lit up her whole face. She was an attractive woman—he could acknowledge that fact without being attracted to her. But looking at her now, he felt the stirring of something low in his belly that he suspected might be attraction.

"Did you at least have a ring?" Rachel asked, as she dipped her fork into the slice of chocolate-raspberry cake that had been set in front of her.

"No. We went to get one the next day." He realized, as he shared the details with Rachel, that it no longer hurt so much to remember the special moments he and Nina had spent together. He'd grieved for his wife for a long time after her quick and unexpected death, but he'd finally accepted that she was gone—that it was time to move on with his life without her.

"I hate being alone on Valentine's Day," Rachel admitted. "But it must be even harder for you—to have found the one person you expected to share your life with, and then lose her."

He shrugged. "Being alone on Valentine's Day isn't really any different from the other three hundred and sixty-four days of the year."

She considered this as she took another sip of her wine, then shook her head. "Logically, I know that's true. And

I'm generally satisfied with my own company. But somehow, on February 14, being single is suddenly spelled A-L-O-N-E, all in capital letters.

"I blame the greeting card companies," she continued. "And the jewelers and chocolate shops—"

"And the florists," he interjected dryly.

She smiled again. "I'm well aware of the hypocrisy. I'm also grateful that the shop keeps me busy so I don't have a lot of time to think about it. But when I lock the door behind the last customer, there's a strange sense of emptiness." She shook her head, as if to shake off the negative thought. "And I just filled that emptiness with too much pasta and bread."

"So let's do something," Andrew suggested impulsively.

She blinked. "What?"

"That was the advice my mother always gave me," he told her. "Don't stew, do."

"Sounds like good advice."

"Are you up for it?" he challenged.

She eyed him with a combination of curiosity and wariness. "I guess that depends on what 'it' is."

He just smiled and called for the check.

Rachel wasn't in the habit of getting into a car with a man she barely knew, especially not heading off to a destination unknown. But Andrew insisted that he wanted to surprise her, and she figured she was safe with him because Gemma and Tony knew him and they knew she was leaving the restaurant with him.

A development that had Gemma's brows rising in silent question when she told her of the plan. Rachel had answered with a shake of her head, warning her friend not to make a big deal out of something that wasn't. She only hoped that she could follow the same advice.

But as he drove toward Ridgemount, she couldn't stop

thinking about the fact that Andrew Garrett—aka Sexy White Roses Guy—was no longer married. And while she understood that his legal status had changed, the fact that he continued to wear his wedding band on his finger confirmed he was still emotionally unavailable.

And that was okay, because she wasn't looking for a relationship. She had no intention of ending her sixteen-month dating hiatus simply because she was in the company of a really hot guy who made her heart pound and her blood hum.

Because somewhere along the line—no doubt when her heart was still bruised over her breakup with Eric—she'd developed a bit of a crush on Andrew Garrett. Her feelings had been fueled, at least in part, by his obvious love for and commitment to his wife. Every time he'd come into the shop, she'd looked at him as proof that there really were good guys in the world. And because she'd believed he was married, she'd been confident that the attraction she felt would never be anything more than an innocent infatuation.

Now that she knew he was widowed, she was afraid that crush might develop into something more. She wasn't looking for anything more, and yet she'd accepted his cryptic challenge. After a brief tussle over the bill—which Gemma settled by refusing to take money from either one of them—she'd chosen to spend time with him rather than go home alone. And after a ten-hour day that left her mentally and physically exhausted, she was a little worried about what that meant.

"Here we are," he said.

Rachel stared at the blinking neon that spelled out Ridgemount Lanes with two crossed pins and a ball between the words.

Apparently "it" was bowling.

He pulled into a parking space and unfastened his seat belt. She didn't move.

"I'm not sure this is a good idea," she told him.

"Why not?"

"Because I can't remember the last time I was bowling." She considered for a minute, her brow furrowed. "Actually, I think it might have been way back in high school."

"How far back is 'way back'?"

"I graduated ten years ago."

"Which means that you're about…twenty-eight?"

Her gaze narrowed. "And you're sneaky."

"Am I right?"

"I'll be twenty-eight at the end of July," she admitted. "How long ago did you graduate high school?"

His smile was wry. "Before you started."

"Another reason we should reconsider this," Rachel told him. "The physical activity might be too strenuous for a man of such advanced age."

"I can handle it if you can," he assured her.

She unfastened her belt.

Before she could reach for the handle of her door, he was there, opening it for her. She followed him through sliding glass panels that parted automatically in response to their approach and was immediately assaulted by unfamiliar noises and scents. The *thunk* of heavy balls dropping onto wood; the crash of pins knocking against each other and toppling over, punctuated by an occasional *whoop* or muttered curse; the smell of lemon polish and French fry grease with a hint of stale sweat.

There were thirty-two lanes, and Rachel was surprised to note that almost half of them were occupied. There were several teams in coordinated shirts that identified them as part of a league, a few groups of teens and several older couples. But the bigger surprise was the discovery of Valentine's decorations hanging from the ceiling: cutouts of cupids' silhouettes and foil hearts, and bouquets of helium-filled heart-shaped balloons at every scoring console.

"So much for forgetting it's February 14," Rachel noted, as she followed Andrew to the counter.

His only response was to ask, "Shoe size?"

"Eight."

The man behind the counter—whose name tag identified him as Grover—had three days' growth of beard, red-rimmed eyes and wore a T-shirt that barely stretched to cover his protruding belly with the inscription: Real Bowlers Play With Their Own Balls. The image effectively killed any romantic ambience and made Rachel feel a lot better about this outing.

"Welcome to Ridgemount Lanes," he said, his voice showcasing slightly more enthusiasm than his tired expression.

"We're going to need a men's twelve, a women's eight and a lane."

"Number Six is available," Grover said. "And just like the Stay Inn, we rent by the hour so you can play as much as you want." He relayed this information with a lewd smile and an exaggerated wink.

Andrew looked at his watch. "There's still two-and-a-half hours of Valentine's Day left," he told Rachel. "Do you want to do two hours?"

She had no idea how much bowling it would take to fill two hours, but since it wouldn't be much of a hardship to spend the time in his company, she said, "Sounds good."

Grover plunked two pairs of shoes down on the counter then punched some buttons on the cash register.

Rachel looked at the battered shoes that were half red and half blue with threadbare black laces, her expression of such horror, Andrew couldn't help but laugh. She picked them up gingerly and held them at arm's length.

She slipped her feet out of the low-heeled boots she was wearing and eased them into the rented footwear. She wiggled her toes then fastened the laces. He programmed their names into the computer, while she took a few steps, testing the shoes.

"Ugly but surprisingly comfortable," she decided.

"You're up first," he told her.

"Why?"

"Because my father taught me that ladies go first."

"But I don't know what I'm doing," she reminded him.

"Take a few practice throws."

She surveyed the selection of balls in the return, finally choosing a pink one. She studied the holes for a minute before sliding her fingers and thumb inside. She took her position on the approach and glanced toward lane ten, where a sixty-something woman strode toward the lane and let her ball fly. It *thunked* on the wood, dangerously close to the gutter, then hooked back toward the middle and crashed into the pins, taking seven of them down.

Andrew watched Rachel square her shoulders, no doubt confident that if the blue-haired lady could do this, she could, too. She took a few tentative steps toward the foul line then bent to release the ball. As she did so, he couldn't help noticing what a nicely shaped derriere she had.

His eyes skimmed downward, appreciating the long, sexy legs encased in snug denim. His gaze moved up again, admiring her distinctly feminine curves, and he felt that stir of something low in his belly again.

When she turned back, her brow was furrowed. She picked up another ball—a blue one this time—and flung it toward the pins. He forced himself to watch the ball rather than her back end and noticed that the blue orb made it about halfway toward the pins before it veered off and into the gutter.

"What am I doing wrong?" she demanded.

"You're turning your wrist."

"No, I'm not."

He shrugged. "Okay, try another one."

She picked up the pink ball again, watched it roll into the gutter, and sighed. "Okay, maybe I am."

"Maybe?"

"But I'm not doing it on purpose."

He stood behind her and wrapped his fingers around her wrist to immobilize it. He felt her pulse racing beneath his fingers and realized that his own heart was beating a little bit faster than usual, too. And when she moved to release the ball, the sweet curve of her bottom brushed against his groin, causing a jolt of lust to spear low in his belly and spread through his veins.

Three pins fell down. She turned around, and the smile that curved her lips illuminated her whole face. "I did it."

"Now do it again."

She picked up the ball with more enthusiasm this time.

"Concentrate on keeping your wrist straight," he told her.

She did so, and knocked down two more pins.

"I think I like this game now," she said, and made him chuckle.

"Ready to get started?" he asked.

"Absolutely," she agreed.

Her enthusiasm waned quickly as she watched Andrew knock down pins with seemingly little effort. But she got a little bit better as the game progressed, although she continued to throw occasional gutter balls. It was near the end of the second game, right after he'd thrown back-to-back strikes, that she eyed him suspiciously.

"Why don't you use any ball except that green one?"

"Because it's the right weight for me."

"Can I try it?"

His brows lifted. "You want to play with my ball?"

Her cheeks flushed. "I want to see if I can knock down more pins with the green ball," she said carefully.

"It's heavier than the one you've been using," he warned.

"You don't think I can handle your ball?" she said, tossing his innuendo back at him.

He handed it to her. "You're welcome to try."

She did—and though she didn't move the ball with much speed, she did manage to knock down six pins. And then she went back to the pink ball.

Andrew didn't comment on her choice. Although he enjoyed the flirtatious banter, he wasn't sure that either of them was ready to follow where a continuation of the conversation might lead.

As the final score was noted, he caught Rachel stifling a yawn. "Sorry," she apologized. "I didn't realize how late it was."

"Did I keep you out past your curfew?" he teased.

She shook her head. "No curfew, but I do have to be at the shop for my flower delivery in the morning."

"What time?"

"Seven."

He winced. "I'm sorry."

"I'm not," she told him. "I had a good time tonight."

"Well, let's turn in those snazzy shoes and get you home."

"You don't have to take me home," she protested. "I can call a cab."

"It's almost midnight—I'm not sending you home in a cab."

"I don't want you to go out of your way." She slipped on her own footwear and picked up the bowling shoes to return them to Grover.

"I won't know if it's out of my way if you won't tell me where you live," he said logically.

"Two-twelve Parkside, just past Queen Street."

He nodded. "I know the area."

They chatted amicably on the drive back to her apartment. When he approached the building, she suggested that he could just drop her off in front. Instead, he parked in an empty spot designated for visitors and walked her to the door.

He didn't follow her into the building, because that might seem too pushy—and too much like a date. Instead, he waited until she'd unlocked the exterior door and said, "Well, I guess I'll see you around."

"Thanks. For a few hours, I actually managed to forget that it was Valentine's Day." Then she impulsively touched her lips to his cheek.

He stood on the step as she went inside and realized that, for the few hours that he'd been with Rachel, he'd forgotten a lot of things—including that holidays without his daughter usually left him feeling sad and lonely and alone. Because he'd felt none of those things with Rachel tonight.

Now he needed to decide whether or not that was a good thing.

Morning came early, but Rachel didn't mind. More than three years after Buds & Blooms had first opened, she still experienced a thrill every time she unlocked the doors, and she still felt like a kid in a candy shop when a delivery of flowers arrived. Today's delivery would be a big one to replenish the stock sold the day before. She was cataloging and sorting various blooms and an assortment of greenery when Holly wandered in at eight—a full two hours before she was scheduled.

Her friend immediately started to prioritize the day's orders then began to gather the necessary containers and flowers.

Rachel let her get organized before she said, "I have

to admit that your early arrival today has me wondering about your date last night."

Holly cut a block of floral foam, stuffed it into a decorative watering can. "It was a disaster."

They worked in silence for a few minutes, until Rachel couldn't take it anymore. "You have to give me more information than that," she protested.

"He made me dinner at his place, with candles and music and wine, and then he asked me to marry him." Her friend cut the stems of a trio of candy-pink gerberas. "Usually I can read guys pretty well, but I did not see that one coming."

Rachel's gaze shifted to Holly's bare left hand. "You turned him down."

"I'm not ready to get married." Holly pushed the stems into the floral foam, then added some pale pink carnations. "And even if I was, I'm not planning to marry someone like Shane."

"So why do you keep dating guys like Shane?"

Her friend sighed. "Because I know I'm not in any danger of falling in love with guys like Shane."

"Too bad Shane didn't know that." And though she knew her friend had done the right thing by turning down his proposal, Rachel couldn't help but feel sorry for the guy.

"But he should have," Holly insisted. "I mean, who proposes marriage to a woman who has carefully avoided any use of the *L*-word?"

"You've been together almost two years—obviously he thought it was implied."

"Except that he's not in love with me, either. He just thought it was the next logical step in our relationship."

"This is why I don't date," Rachel told her. "Because a few dates eventually lead to a relationship and one party or another ends up with a broken heart."

"I should have come over to your place last night for the *Criminal Minds* marathon."

"Actually, I wasn't home last night."

Her friend pushed the finished watering can arrangement aside. "Where were you?"

"Bowling."

"By yourself?"

"No." She plucked the wilted blooms out of a container and tossed them into the garbage. "With Andrew Garrett."

Holly frowned. "Sexy White Roses Guy?"

Rachel nodded.

"The one with the wedding ring on his finger?" her friend pressed.

"He's widowed."

"Oh." Holly considered for a minute. "How long?"

"Three years."

"And he still wears the ring?"

Rachel shrugged.

Holly counted out eight white lilies. "I didn't know you bowled."

"I don't."

"So how did this come about?"

"We were both at Valentino's for eat-in takeout, and the next thing I knew, I was wearing ugly shoes."

"That's probably why you don't bowl," Holly noted. "The shoes offend your impeccable sense of style."

"And yet, I had a good time."

"Because you enjoyed the game—or because you enjoyed being with Sexy White Roses Guy?"

"He is sexy," Rachel acknowledged. "And charming and interesting and funny."

"Uh-oh."

She frowned. "Uh-oh—what?"

"One date and you're falling for him already."

"It wasn't a date and I'm not falling for him."

Holly didn't look convinced. "I'm all for you finally ending your ridiculous dating hiatus, but I don't want you getting hung up on somebody else who isn't available."

"I'm not hung up on him."

"You went bowling with him—and you don't bowl."

Rachel sighed. "Our options were limited."

"Did he kiss you?"

"It wasn't a date."

"That wouldn't stop most guys I know from making a move," her friend noted. "Then again, most guys I know don't wear wedding bands—even the ones who are married."

Rachel waited until her friend finished then she said, "Actually, I kissed him."

"What?"

"It was a thank-you," she explained. "An impulse."

"Was there tongue?"

She rolled her eyes. "I touched my lips to his cheek."

"Oh." Holly sounded disappointed. "I'm not sure that even counts as a kiss."

"Then I guess I didn't kiss him."

"When you kissed him, did you feel those little flutters in your belly?"

"Make up your mind—did I kiss him or not?"

"That depends on whether or not there were flutters."

There had been definite flutters, and her heart had raced and her knees had gone weak. But she wasn't prepared to admit any of that to her friend.

"Customer," she said, when the bell over the door jangled.

"We're not done with this conversation," Holly warned.

But more customers kept her busy in the front of the shop so that Holly was unable to continue her interrogation. And when Rachel left work at two o'clock, she was confident that she'd kept the truth about her feelings for Andrew Garrett to herself.

Chapter Three

Saturday afternoon, Andrew was in his home workshop assembling a sideboard when his middle brother stopped by.

Nathan walked around the piece, giving it a thorough examination. "Nice—but not your usual style."

"It's for Ed and Carol's dining room." The Wakefields were his in-laws—or maybe they were former in-laws. Andrew wasn't sure if the death of his wife changed the relationship between himself and her parents. Either way, they were still his daughter's grandparents.

"Don't they know that you're the VP of Product Research and Design for a multibillion-dollar furniture company now and not just a carpenter?"

"I'm still a carpenter," Andrew insisted. "A fancy title doesn't change that."

"And a damn good one," Nate agreed, continuing his inspection of the work. "Is this an original design?"

He nodded. "Ed wanted something special for Carol, for their fortieth anniversary."

"When's that?"

"Not until October. But I had the time now, so I figured I'd get started."

"Mom and Dad's fortieth is in May," Nathan reminded him. "And Mom wants a party."

"She always wants a party. Do you remember Maura's first birthday? She invited sixty people."

"It was a kick-ass first birthday," his brother agreed.

"I can only imagine how many people she'll invite to a fortieth wedding anniversary."

"Apparently we're supposed to do the inviting."

"Huh?"

Nate nodded. "She said that proper etiquette requires the party be hosted by someone other than the anniversary couple. Preferably the couple's children."

"Not if she wants it done right," Andrew noted.

"Daniel suggested we hire an event planner."

"Not a bad idea," he admitted. "And since it was his idea, he should look into that."

Nate went to the mini-fridge and took out a couple of beers. He twisted the caps off both, then handed one to his brother. "Speaking of anniversaries—I stopped by last night."

Andrew tipped the bottle to his lips. "So...today is the twenty-four-hour anniversary of your visit?"

"Okay, I guess that wasn't a very good segue."

"What are you trying to segue into?"

"Asking where you were last night."

"Did we have plans that I forgot about?"

"No—but it was Valentine's Day."

Andrew slapped his hand to his forehead. "And I didn't even get you a card."

"You're a funny guy," Nate said, his tone devoid of amusement.

"Yes, it was Valentine's Day," he agreed. "And Maura

was with the Wakefields and I was hungry, so I went to Valentino's to grab a bite to eat. I ran into someone I know, so we had dinner together and then went bowling."

"I assume this 'someone' you know is female?"

"Yes, she's female. No, it wasn't a date."

"You've grieved long enough," Nathan told him.

"I'm not still grieving," Andrew told him. "Yeah, I still miss Nina sometimes—" which was a vast improvement over the "all the time" that he'd missed her and looked for her in the first year after her death. "But it's not like I've put my life on hold."

"It's exactly like you've put your life on hold," his brother countered. "Or is there another explanation for the fact that you haven't had a relationship with anyone else since Nina died?"

"I've been on dates," he protested, although they both knew that he'd only been out a handful of times since his wife's death—the first being only about six months ago.

"A few first dates and not a single second date."

He shrugged. "I haven't met anyone that I wanted to go out with more than once."

Even as Andrew said the words, a carousel of images played through his mind—and all of them were Rachel. Behind the counter of the flower shop, a small smile on her face as she wrapped a bouquet; in the kitchen at Valentino's, a hint of sadness clouding her gorgeous blue eyes when she mentioned her dating hiatus; at the bowling alley, a brilliant smile illuminating her face after she'd knocked down her first pins; outside her apartment building at the end of the night, her eyes soft and warm, as her lips touched his cheek.

"What about Bridget?"

He pushed the memories of Rachel to the back of his mind. "Bridget was serious stalker material."

"What did she do—call you the day after your date?"

"She called. She texted. She emailed. And then she showed up at the house—and I never told her where I lived."

"Okay, that's a little obsessive," Nathan allowed.

"And when I made the mistake of inviting her to come inside for a drink—because I didn't know how else to respond to her presence on my doorstep—she immediately started making decorating suggestions."

"Well, she is an interior designer."

"Who walked through the house until she found my bedroom and then told me the feng shui wasn't conducive to getting naked and sweaty."

Nate winced. "Okay—forget Bridget. Tell me about this girl you went bowling with last night—how did you meet her?"

"She works at a flower shop downtown."

"Please don't tell me you were in there buying flowers to take to the cemetery."

"Okay, I won't tell you."

Nathan groaned. "That's pathetic."

"Why does it matter where I met her? We're just... friends," he decided, because acquaintances seemed overly vague a description for a woman who had played a starring role in the sexual dreams that plagued his sleep the previous evening. Of course, he wasn't going to share that with his brother.

"Is she coyote ugly?"

He choked on his beer. "Jeez, Nate. No. She's not ugly at all."

"Then what does she look like?"

He could picture her clearly: the silky brown hair that she kept tied back when she was working but had brushed out so that it hung loose to her shoulders last night; the deep blue eyes that reminded him of clear summer skies; the light dusting of freckles over the bridge of her pert nose; the tiny mole at the corner of her temptingly shaped mouth; the graceful slope of her shoulders; the unmistakably feminine curves.

But he couldn't mention any one of those things, because he knew that if he did, his brother would somehow sense everything that he wasn't saying. Most notably that Rachel Ellis was the first woman who had stuck in his mind—and stirred his body—in a very long time.

"She's...attractive," he finally said. "In a girl-next-door kind of way."

Nathan's brows lifted. "So if you're really not interested, maybe you'll introduce her to me."

"No." His response was immediate and unequivocal.

"Why not?"

"Because she's...sweet."

"I like sweet."

"Said the wolf to Red Riding Hood," Andrew noted drily.

His brother grinned.

"Besides, I thought you were dating some flight attendant."

"Yeah, but since she picked up the San Francisco to Tokyo route, I hardly see her," he admitted.

"I guess that would explain why you were alone on Valentine's Day."

"And most other days that end with a *y*," Nate grumbled.

Before Andrew could respond to that, his brother's pocket started ringing. Nate pulled out his cell phone and smiled when he saw the name on the display. Andrew started to clear up his tools while his brother answered the call.

"That was Mallory," he said, tucking his phone away again. "She's got four days off and is just about to get on a plane headed home."

"I guess you're not going to be alone tonight," he noted.

His brother grinned. "Do you know where I can pick up some flowers?"

Maura didn't understand why they had to go outside for recess. Mrs. Patterson, her first grade teacher, insisted that fresh air was good for them. But by the time they all got their boots and hats and coats on, recess was half-over.

Sometimes they played grounders on the climber, but today she was just hanging out on the swings with her best friend, Kristy. Not even swinging, just sitting on the cold plastic seats and waiting for the bell to ring again so they could go back inside.

"I saw Simon put a Valentine in your box on Friday."

"He gave Valentines to everyone," Maura said. "It's like a rule."

"But he gave you the biggest one," Kristy said. "I think he likes you."

Maura just shrugged. Kristy thought it was a big deal to know which boys liked which girls, but she didn't really care.

"Boys give you things when they like you—especially on Valentine's Day," Kristy told her. "My mom's boyfriend gave her a ring and now they're going to get married and Greg's going to be my new dad."

"But you already have a dad."

"Yeah, but my mom says he's a deadbeat and Greg will be a better one."

Maura frowned. It didn't seem fair that Kristy was getting another dad when she already had one. Not that Maura wanted another dad—she already had the best dad in the world. But she thought it would be kinda cool if she could get a new mom, 'cuz the one she'd had died when Maura was little.

"And I get to be a flower girl in the wedding," Kristy

said. "But Tiffany gets to be a bridesmaid, 'cuz she's older and 'cuz she got to be a flower girl at our mom's last wedding. We're gonna have matching dresses, though. Probably pink."

Maura thought it would be fun to be in a wedding. Before Christmas, her dad had taken her out of school for a couple of days so they could go to Uncle Jack's wedding. Her cousin, Ava, was a bridesmaid, and she got to walk down the aisle of the church just like the bride.

Knowing that Kristy was going to be in a wedding, Maura felt something curl in her belly. It was what her daddy called a green-eyed monster. She knew it wasn't really a monster, but the bad feeling she got when she wanted what someone else had. She should be happy that Kristy was going to be in a wedding, but she wished she could be in a wedding, too.

And it really wasn't fair that Kristy was gonna have two dads and she didn't even have one mom.

Rachel flipped the page on the calendar when she opened up the shop Saturday morning. It was March 1st—two weeks after Valentine's Day. And in that time, she hadn't seen or heard from Andrew Garrett again. Which wasn't at all unusual. In fact, if he stuck to his usual pattern, she wouldn't see him again until August.

So while it wasn't surprising that he hadn't come by the shop, it was disappointing. She'd thought—hoped—that the time they'd spent together on Valentine's Day might have meant something to him. Because it had meant something to her. The fact that he hadn't made any effort to contact her since suggested otherwise.

She'd tried to put the events of that evening out of her mind as completely as he'd apparently done. But sometimes her thoughts would wander and she'd remember the surprising camaraderie they'd shared for a few hours—and the even more surprising tug of attraction.

There was something about the man that really appealed to her—and turned on parts of her that had been turned off for a very long time. Unfortunately, the attraction she felt was obviously one-sided. As Holly had pointed out, date or no date, if a guy was interested, he made a move. Andrew hadn't made a move—he hadn't even responded to her move.

If, that is, kissing a guy on the cheek could be considered a move and not just an impulse to express her gratitude for a fun evening. And maybe, subconsciously, she'd also been testing the waters a little.

The combination of his enticing masculine scent and the faint shadow of stubble on his jaw had been as intoxicating as the wine she'd enjoyed with her dinner. And when her lips had brushed his raspy cheek, she'd felt the tingles all the way down to her toes.

Sixteen months was a long time to go without dating—and everything else it entailed. The brief contact had her suddenly yearning for that everything else, and tempted her to dive right in. Andrew, on the other hand, had given no indication that he even wanted to get his feet wet.

She tried to put him out of her mind. It was ridiculous to spend so much time thinking about a man she barely knew. A man who, as Holly had pointed out, was probably still in love with and grieving for his deceased wife. Unfortunately that knowledge didn't change the fact that, two weeks after their Valentine's Day non-date, she hadn't stopped thinking about him.

On the plus side, two weeks after Holly's Valentine's Day breakup, she wasn't yet dating anyone new, so she and Rachel were hanging out more often. In fact, today Trish was coming in at lunch to manage the shop so they could head to Raleigh to catch an afternoon basketball game. But first they had to finish up the last of the centerpieces for Holly's grandmother's ninetieth birthday party the following day.

They were on the last one—Rachel cutting and Holly arranging—when Holly's phone chimed to indicate a text message. She frowned at the screen.

"Problem?" Rachel asked.

"I don't know—it's a cryptic bunch of letters and numbers from Gary."

Gary was Holly's brother, currently in England to finish up a Master's Degree at the London School of Economics. "Letters and numbers?"

"'BA5521 15:40 can u pick up?'" As she read the message out loud, Holly's eyes widened. "Ohmygod. It's flight information."

"He's coming home for your grandmother's birthday party," Rachel guessed.

Her friend's eyes filled with tears as she typed a reply. "He didn't come home for Christmas. I haven't seen him since August."

Rachel passed her a tissue. "You'll see him this afternoon."

"I'll see him this afternoon." Her lips curved in anticipation of the reunion, then her smile slipped. "Oh, Rachel, I'm sorry."

She shook her head. "Don't you dare apologize."

"But you already bought the tickets."

"So I'll find someone else to go with me—or I won't. It's not a big deal."

"Are you sure? Because I could ask one of my cousins to—"

"I'm sure," Rachel interjected. "Your brother coming home is a big deal—you need to be there."

Holly nodded her thanks.

Rachel started transferring the finished centerpieces

to the fridge while her friend swept the cuttings from the table. When the front door chimed, Rachel's hands were full of flowers and Trish wasn't in yet, so Holly went to the front of the shop to assist the customer. Thirty seconds later, she was back again and nudging her business partner toward the showroom.

Though Rachel was puzzled by her friend's odd behavior, she didn't ask any questions. It wouldn't be the first time Holly had chosen to hide out in the back rather than face an ex-boyfriend who had ventured into the shop. With her polite smile in place, she moved out past the counter—and found herself face-to-face with Andrew Garrett.

"Mr. Garrett. Hi."

He smiled, and her already wildly pounding heart kicked it up another notch.

"I thought we were on a first-name basis now," he said to her.

Were they? She didn't know what to think, why he was there. But she couldn't deny that she was really glad to see him. "Andrew," she amended. "How can I help you today?"

"What kind of flowers would you recommend to express a heartfelt and sincere apology?"

She felt a smile tug at the corners of her mouth. "How badly did you screw up?"

"You tell me."

"Sorry?"

"That's supposed to be my line," he said. "And I *am* sorry."

"Why?" she asked cautiously.

"Because I couldn't decide whether or not I should call, and when I finally admitted to myself that I wanted to call, I realized I didn't have your number. By then, a whole week had passed so I figured there was no point in tracking you down because you'd probably already written me off. And now it's two weeks later, but I haven't stopped thinking about you, so here I am anyway."

"You're here to see *me?*"

He nodded. "Obviously you're working right now, but if you don't object to giving me your number, maybe I can call you sometime and we could make plans to do something again?"

She took one of the business cards from the holder by the cash register and was scribbling her home number on it when Holly came through from the back with a spring assortment to set in the display case.

"I'm sorry for reneging on our plans this afternoon," Holly said to Rachel. And then, as if she'd only now realized that Andrew was there, "Oh—I didn't realize you were with a customer."

Rachel rolled her eyes in response to the blatant fib. "Holly, this is Andrew Garrett. Andrew, my friend and business partner, Holly Kendrick."

"I apologize for interrupting," Holly said to him. "I just got a message that my brother's coming into town so I have to pick him up from the airport, but I feel terrible about abandoning Rachel with two tickets to a Wolfpack game on a Saturday afternoon."

"Shouldn't you be on your way to the airport now?" Rachel suggested.

"You're right," Holly agreed. "It was nice meeting you, Andrew. See you tomorrow, Rachel." Then she disappeared into the back again and—hopefully—out the back door.

"Was that your friend's not-so-subtle way of letting me know that you don't have any plans today?" Andrew asked when Holly had gone.

"Actually that was subtle, at least for Holly. And I do have plans."

"The basketball game."

She nodded.

"I like basketball," he said. "If you wanted to sell the extra ticket to me, I'd go with you."

"I'm not selling the ticket to you," she told him. "But I will let you buy the popcorn."

He smiled. "Sounds fair. What time's the game?"

"Four o'clock."

"I'll pick you up at two-thirty."

Andrew pressed the code to buzz Rachel's apartment at precisely two-thirty. After he identified himself over the intercom, she told him "apartment 704" and released the lock.

He stepped into the lobby and took a moment to look around while he waited for the elevator. He'd never lived in an apartment and wasn't sure he could do so without feeling claustrophobic, but he had to admit that this building had ambience. There were watercolors on the walls, fresh flowers strategically placed around the room and leather seating around a gas fireplace.

A quiet *ding* indicated the elevator's arrival and, a minute later, he was at Rachel's door. She responded promptly to his knock.

"I just need to grab my purse," she said, and stepped back so that he could enter.

He didn't glance around her apartment because his gaze was riveted on her. She'd changed from her work clothes into a pair of black jeans that molded to her narrow hips and a soft pink sweater that hugged her curves and somehow made her eyes seem even bluer. She'd brushed her hair out, so that it spilled over her shoulders in a silky cloud. On her feet she wore black boots with heels that looked more fashionable than practical.

He felt a distinctive tug low in his groin and couldn't deny it was attraction. And his body's instinctive response to Rachel Ellis worried him, because he sensed that there was something more going on here than basic chemistry. Lust was simple enough, but what he felt for Rachel wasn't simple. There was something more mixed with the desire he felt, and he was concerned that he could—maybe already did—actually like her.

She picked up her purse off the console, double-checked that she had the tickets, then grabbed her coat from the closet. "Okay," she told him.

When he didn't shift from his position in front of the door, she looked up at him. He watched her eyes darken as puzzlement changed to awareness, and the pulse at the base of her throat quickened as awareness gave way to desire. It had been a long time since he'd had to read a woman's signals, but he was confident that the attraction he felt was reciprocated.

She moistened her lips with the tip of her tongue. "Are you, uh, ready?"

"Yeah," he agreed. "There's just one thing I think we should get out of the way before we go."

And then he kissed her.

Chapter Four

Oh. My. God.

He was kissing her.

And this wasn't a casual brush of the lips. It was immediate and full mouth-on-mouth contact. Not in a way that could be considered aggressive or pushy, just direct and sure, and there was something incredibly sexy about his self-confidence.

In the space of a heartbeat, those masterful lips took Rachel from casually intrigued to completely aroused. About three seconds later, she decided that if levels of expertise could be assessed like in the martial arts, he was a black-belt grand master of kissing. Two seconds after that, she was incapable of forming any other coherent thoughts.

Kissing Andrew Garrett was simply…bliss.

He lifted a hand to cup the nape of her neck, his thumb gently brushing over the racing pulse point below her jaw. His other arm curled around her back, drawing her closer. She went willingly, eagerly. Her lips parted beneath the pressure of his, and when his tongue slipped between them, she felt the surge of heat through her veins, igniting flames of desire.

And still he continued to kiss her, savoring the taste and texture of her mouth without pressing for anything more. His lips nibbled, his tongue teased and everything inside of her quivered with want, need. He wanted her, too—there was no mistaking the desire she tasted in his kiss—but it was tempered by patience, balanced by caution.

Because she had her own reasons for being careful, she appreciated his restraint. But she was still disappointed when he finally lifted his mouth from hers.

She was twenty-seven years old. She'd had boyfriends, relationships, heartbreaks. She'd shared her body and her bed with other men, but never had any other man kissed her with the focused intensity Andrew demonstrated. Even now, he kept his arm around her, as if he wasn't quite ready to let her go.

"I've been thinking about that since Valentine's Day," he told her.

"Oh. Um." The power of conversation had completely deserted her along with the ability to form coherent thoughts.

He smiled. "Yeah, I know the feeling."

"I wasn't— I'm not—" She blew out a breath. "I'm on a dating hiatus."

"You mentioned that."

"And we're supposed to be going to the basketball game."

"That's why I'm here."

"I'm a really big Wolfpack fan."

"Okay," he agreed.

"But now I'm thinking…that I might want to *not* see the game even more."

The glint of humor in his green eyes faded; the arm around her waist tightened. "Rachel."

"I'm not usually the impulsive type, and I don't even really know you. Or maybe it's just that sixteen months is a really long time to go without having sex. Except that I didn't even think about it for most of that time, and all you did was kiss me, but I'm definitely thinking about it now."

"I'm thinking about it, too," he admitted.

"But we had a deal," she reminded him.

"We did?"

She nodded. "You're buying the popcorn."

"Popcorn. Right." He finally released her and took a step back. "Then I guess we should be going."

She felt a little bit steadier as they waited for the elevator. Although there was no one else in the hall, she was confident that she had enough self-restraint to refrain from tearing his clothes off in a public place. And when the doors of the elevator closed behind them, she was sure the moment of insanity had passed.

The blast of cold air that greeted her when they exited the building quickly cooled her heated skin. In fact, she'd only taken a few steps before she was wishing that she'd grabbed a hat and gloves. Instead, she stuffed her hands into the pockets of her jacket and tucked her chin deeper into the collar to combat the unseasonably cold weather. When her heel caught a patch of ice, she would have fallen onto her butt if Andrew hadn't managed to catch her elbow and hold her up.

"I was right," he murmured.

"About what?"

"Your boots are more stylish than practical."

"I wear the practical ones every day," she told him. "I like to dress up a little when I go out."

"Did I mention how nice you look?"

"Not in so many words, but I thought the kiss might have been an indicator."

"I'm usually pretty good with words, but it's been a long time since I've done the dating thing," he said apologetically, as he walked around to the passenger door of his car.

She had no complaints about his communication skills, but she didn't dare say so in case he interpreted her response as an invitation to kiss her again. Not that she would object if he did so, she just wasn't sure she could handle another one of his kisses right now.

"I should have said that you look nice—beautiful, actually."

It wasn't the smoothest compliment she'd ever received, but she could tell that he meant it, and despite the fact that her teeth were close to chattering, she felt her cheeks heat.

He opened the door for her.

She lowered herself onto the leather seat and reached for the belt. Andrew slid in behind the steering wheel and started the car, immediately turning up the temperature. Before he had pulled out of the parking lot, she could feel the warm air on her frigid feet.

As the heat permeated the vehicle and thawed her extremities, she became aware of other things: the wide-palmed hands wrapped around the steering wheel, the breadth of his shoulders beneath his leather jacket, the strong line of his jaw darkened with just the slightest hint of stubble and the clean, masculine scent of him that filled her nostrils every time she drew a breath. She definitely wasn't feeling cold anymore, not with all of the heat churning inside of her.

She unfastened the top two buttons of her coat, and he automatically reached for the button to adjust the climate control. She mentally added *courteous* to his already-impressive list of attributes that included handsome, charming, loyal—and a fabulous kisser.

In fact, her head was still reeling from that kiss. Ordinarily such a bold move would have put her off. But it was hard to be annoyed when every long-dormant nerve ending in her body was standing at attention and begging for more.

"So how did you become a Wolfpack fan?" he asked her.

"My brother played college basketball."

"At NC State?"

She nodded. "Did you ever play?"

"No, my game was football. At Duke."

She might have guessed football, because of those shoulders. But he was tall enough that basketball wouldn't have been out of the question. The school, however, surprised her. "Both Holly and I went to Duke."

He smiled. "I think we've already established that I would have been there a lot of years before you."

"Unless it took you a long time to graduate," she teased.

He laughed. "I got the standard four-year degree in four years."

She had a lot more questions, but he turned the focus back to her. "Did you meet Holly at college?"

"No, we go way back to the second grade when Holly's parents split up and she and her brother came to Charisma to live with her grandmother. We first decided we would go into business together when we were in fifth grade, but we didn't know the business was going to be flowers."

"How did that come about?"

"We both majored in business, but Holly liked to try a lot of different things and occasionally took courses just for fun. One of those was a floral-design class offered on Saturday mornings, and she fell in love with it."

"So you're the 'Buds' of Buds & Blooms," he realized. "Clever."

"We thought so," she agreed. "Most people assume 'Buds' is a reference to undeveloped flowers—and it is. But we liked that it was also an abbreviation of buddies."

And since she'd already told him far more than she intended, she said, "So tell me about you—what do you do?"

"Nothing very exciting," he warned.

"You mean you're not a NASA astronaut or government spy?"

He chuckled. "Unfortunately, no. I'm a carpenter."

Which explained his strong and confident hands. "What kind of carpentry do you do?

"Mostly finish work and cabinetry."

"So you're a detail man," she surmised.

"I guess that's a fair assessment." He turned into the parking lot of PNC Arena.

"Do you like your work?"

"Most days."

"Then you're doing the right thing."

The parking lot was rapidly filling up, so he drove directly to the gate. "Why don't you get out here and I'll meet you inside after I've parked the car?"

"Okay," she agreed, and added *chivalrous* to the ever-growing list she was compiling. Obviously his mother had raised him to treat a girl right—and this girl's heart was already starting to go pitter-patter.

It's just a basketball game, she reminded herself. Not a date. He was only there with her because Holly had bailed and Rachel happened to have an extra ticket. And she might almost have believed this was just an impromptu outing between casual acquaintances, except for that kiss.

She had to stop thinking about that kiss.

Because every minute that she spent with him, she found him more attractive and appealing, and she wasn't looking for any kind of romantic involvement at this point in her life. She wasn't ready to end her dating hiatus just yet. She didn't want to feel all the feelings he stirred up inside her. In fact, she almost hoped that he would shove popcorn into his mouth by the handful or slurp on his soda or send text messages throughout the game so that she could focus on some annoying behavior and stop thinking about the feel of his mouth on hers.

He shouldn't have kissed her.

Not that Andrew regretted the off-the-charts lip-lock they'd shared, but he knew it would have been smarter to resist the impulse that urged him to sample the taste and texture of her temptingly curved mouth. Because now he couldn't think about anything but the softness of her lips, the sweet flavor of her and the surprising passion in her response.

And no matter how many times he told himself that what he'd shared with Rachel was just a kiss, he wasn't reassured. Because now he wanted to kiss her again and again, and he wanted those kisses to lead to more. A lot more.

He spotted her immediately when he walked through the doors. She was standing just inside, waiting for him. He wondered how it was that he'd been into her shop more than half a dozen times over the past few years, had several conversations with her and never noticed how truly beautiful she was.

Sure, he'd felt a subtle buzz, but until their paths had crossed at Valentino's two weeks ago, he'd never seen her as anything other than the woman who worked at the flower shop. Maybe, prior to that day, he hadn't been ready to see her as anything more.

Her lips curved when she spotted him, and his gaze automatically dipped to the soft, sweet mouth. There was no doubt he was feeling the attraction now.

"Popcorn?" he asked.

"Absolutely," she agreed.

He bought a large popcorn and a couple of drinks, then they went to find their seats.

The last time he'd been at the arena was with Maura. A guy at work had a couple of tickets to a Hurricanes game that he couldn't use, so he gave them to Andrew. And they were great seats, too.

His daughter, unfortunately, had been less than thrilled with the close-up view of players ruthlessly crushed against the glass. And when a little bit of jostling ended with the gloves dropping and fists pumping, she'd started to cry. They'd left before the end of the second period.

Thinking about Maura at that game reminded him that he hadn't mentioned his daughter to Rachel.

He wasn't deliberately keeping the existence of his child a secret from her—he just hadn't yet found a way to bring her name into the conversation. Maybe he hadn't tried too hard, but, truthfully, he was enjoying talking about other things for a change. The basic getting-to-know-one-another conversations always seemed to take on a different tone whenever he revealed that he was a single father.

Some women weren't interested in playing mommy to another woman's child, but in Andrew's recent and admittedly limited dating experience, most of them tried to use the existence of his motherless child to worm their way into his affections.

He didn't disagree that a child needed a mother, and he felt fortunate that both his mother and his former mother-in-law were close to Maura. He also had three female cousins who doted on his little girl, so she had plenty of women in her life. And although a couple of his dates had expressed an interest in meeting his daughter, none of them had ever done so.

It was too early to decide whether or not Rachel would be the first, but if he planned to see her again after tonight, he knew that he had to tell her about Maura. Not now—not in the midst of a crowded arena only minutes before the game was scheduled to start, but definitely before their relationship progressed further than a few kisses.

As the players continued their warm-ups, he glanced over at Rachel and discovered that the low V-neckline of her soft pink sweater afforded him a tempting view of pale skin and a hint of shadowy cleavage.

He shifted uncomfortably in his seat. The initial attraction to Rachel had been nothing more than a mild curiosity, a subtle stirring in his blood. Then they'd had dinner together on Valentine's Day, and they'd talked and laughed and he'd realized he actually liked her. That, combined with the attraction, changed everything for him. Or maybe it was the first kiss—the impulsive touch of her lips to his cheek. But somewhere along the line, what had started as a subtle stirring in his blood had escalated to a raging hunger, so that he actually ached with wanting her.

Was it simply a matter of timing? Was he finally ready to move on with his life? Or was it Rachel? Was there something about this specific woman that got to him?

He reached for more popcorn, and his fingers brushed over the back of her hand. The casual touch sent heat coursing through his veins, and the little catch in her breath confirmed that she'd felt something, too. Her gaze lifted to his, her blue eyes wide, aware. Her slightly parted lips glistened with butter, tempting him to lick it away.

The sound of a buzzer made both of them jump, and he forced his attention back to the court.

Two hours later, as they merged with the crowd exiting the arena, Andrew wasn't ready to take Rachel home. His house was always so empty and quiet when Maura was gone, and he wasn't eager to get back to it. Not that either *empty* or *quiet* had ever bothered him too much before— he was usually content with his own company. But today he was enjoying being with Rachel a lot more.

"Are you hungry?" he asked. "Did you want to go somewhere to grab a bite to eat?"

"I should say I'm not after all of that popcorn, but it would be a lie."

"You burned off a lot of calories in that game," he said, teasing her about her inability to sit still while watching the action.

"No one's ever accused me of being passive," she admitted.

It was an innocent remark, but that didn't prevent his imagination from running with it and wondering if she would demonstrate the same energy in the bedroom.

"So—" he cleared his throat "—you up for O'Reilly's?"

It would probably be smarter to decline his invitation. Sitting beside him at the arena, Rachel had been so hyperaware of every brush of his thigh and touch of his hand that she'd found it difficult to concentrate on what was happening in the game. Apparently sixteen months without sex had turned her into a mass of quivering hormones, and she was afraid that spending more time with him might be too much temptation for her to resist.

And she had reason to be wary. She didn't know very much about him aside from the fact that her heart pounded a little bit faster whenever he was near. And despite the kiss they'd shared—all she had to do was think about that kiss and her blood started to heat—she didn't want to get involved with a man who was still in love with his late wife.

His devotion to the woman he'd married was admirable, and she respected that. But Rachel also knew that, for her, the same loyalty and commitment could mean heartbreak. Of course, he'd only asked her if she wanted to get some food, not to move in with him, so she nodded.

"Sounds good."

The blast of cold air that hit her when they exited

the building made her shiver, and he slid his arm across her shoulders, tucking her close to his body to share his warmth. The action immediately succeeded. Every place that their bodies were in contact—even through several layers of clothes—she felt heat.

The intensity of the attraction she felt for this man was more than a little unnerving. She wasn't looking to get involved right now. Although business was doing well, Buds & Blooms took most of her time and attention. More than once, Holly had accused Rachel of burying herself in work to avoid heartbreak, and she couldn't deny that there was probably some truth to that claim.

The end of her relationship with Eric had left scars that she wasn't sure were completely healed. She'd been in love and believed that they were planning a life and a future together. But he'd already found the one woman he would love forever, and it had taken Rachel a long time to realize that woman wasn't her. His daughter was just one more factor in the already-complicated equation that centered around his ex-wife.

When she'd finally figured things out and walked away, he'd tried to change her mind. But he'd been unwilling to make any changes in his life. Wendy still called the shots and, because he was still in love with her, he let her. And that made their relationship a little too crowded for Rachel's liking.

Andrew had his share of baggage, evidenced by the gold band he still wore on the third finger of his left hand. But at least his wife was no longer telling him what to do and when to do it.

Still, it was reason to be cautious. After sixteen months of not dating, she wasn't going to dive headfirst into another relationship potentially fraught with similar problems. But she couldn't deny that she was tempted.

* * *

O'Reilly's was a traditional Irish pub with lots of dark wood, shadowy lighting and regular patrons lined up on stools at the bar drinking any of the dozen different beers on tap.

Andrew led her to a narrow booth with padded vinyl benches and helped her with her coat. When they were seated, a waitress hurried over to their table. She was blonde, built and beautiful—and she hauled Andrew out of the booth and gave him a smacking kiss on the lips.

"Jeez." He wiped his hand over his mouth. "Can't you see I'm with someone?"

"I can," she agreed, winking at Rachel. "I just don't believe it."

"And there went your tip, right out the door." He turned to Rachel. "I'd like to apologize for my cousin. I wouldn't have suggested we come here if I'd known she was working today."

"Jordyn Garrett," the waitress said.

Rachel shook her proffered hand. "Rachel Ellis."

"It's a pleasure to meet you," Jordyn said. "And now I can tell the rest of the family that I was the first to meet Andrew's new girlfriend."

"Oh, I'm not… I mean, this isn't…" She looked helplessly at Andrew.

He just shrugged. "Don't worry about it—you won't dissuade Jordyn from believing what she wants to believe."

His cousin just grinned. "So, are you here for food or drinks or both?"

"Both," Andrew said.

"Tell me what you want to drink and I'll go grab a couple of menus."

He looked at Rachel. She wasn't much of a beer drinker, so she asked for a shandy; Andrew ordered a Guinness, and the waitress went to get their beverages.

While they were in the arena, Rachel had the distraction of the game to focus on. Now, even though there were plenty of other customers in the restaurant, she felt as if she was alone with him. Or maybe it was Jordyn's teasing that had somehow turned their casual outing into a date and caused the butterflies to start winging around in her tummy.

They accepted Jordyn's recommendation of the potato cakes as their appetizer, and Rachel decided to try the cottage pie for her main course while Andrew opted for the lamb stew.

The pub was doing a brisk business and there were only two waitresses on duty, so Jordyn was kept busy— or maybe she was just giving them space. She checked in periodically, offering refills on drinks and ensuring they were satisfied with their meals, but she didn't hover.

She suggested coffee after dinner, which they both accepted, and dessert, which they both declined. When their cups were empty and the bill was settled—this time Jordyn let him win the battle over payment—Andrew again left Rachel waiting inside the warmth of the pub while he went to get the car.

"Are you working tomorrow?" he asked, when they were finally headed back to her apartment.

She shook her head. "Trish and Elaine are in charge tomorrow so that Holly and I can both attend her grandmother's ninetieth birthday party."

"The same grandmother she came to live with when she was in second grade?"

She nodded. "And because I spent so much time with Holly and all of my grandparents live in other parts of the country, Phoebe sort of adopted me as one of her own."

"Are your parents still in town?"

"No, they retired to Arizona a few years back."

"Any siblings besides the basketball player?"

"Just Rick. He lives in Raleigh with his wife and two little boys."

He turned into the parking lot of her apartment building and found a vacant spot in the designated visitors' section. "How old are your nephews?"

"Five and seven."

"Do you spend much time with them?"

"As much as I can and still not nearly enough." She unbuckled her seat belt and reached for the handle of the door. Of course, he was already out of the car and opening it for her.

"You don't have to walk me to the door," she protested.

"My mother would be appalled if I didn't," he told her.

"I won't tell if you won't."

"She has ways of finding things out."

She slid her key into the exterior lock. "Your parents live in Charisma?"

"My parents and two younger brothers, along with a few aunts and uncles and numerous cousins besides Jordyn."

This time he followed her into the building and to the elevator.

She wanted to know more about him and his family, but once the elevator doors closed, she was suddenly conscious of being alone with him again. And all the way up to the seventh floor, she wondered if he was going to kiss her again.

She hoped he would. And she told herself that she would be ready for it this time. But being prepared for his kiss did nothing to lessen the impact.

The brush of his mouth against hers caused tingles of awareness to dance over her skin. The slide of his hands around her back made her heart pound and her body ache. And when his tongue swirled around hers, her bones turned to jelly. Her hands were on his shoulders, holding on to him for balance as the world spun around her. And still he continued to kiss her.

No, it wasn't just a kiss—it was a seduction. He was seducing her with nothing more than a kiss. A mind-scrambling, body-numbing kiss.

She wasn't the type of woman to jump into bed with a man she barely knew. At least she'd never been so before. But she was hovering on the brink of inviting Andrew to come inside. Her hands slid off his shoulders and he linked them with his. The twining of their fingers together, the slide of his palm against hers was incredibly erotic. Oh, how she wanted to feel those hands on her body.

Then he squeezed her hands gently, and she felt the cool, hard metal of the band around the third finger of his left hand.

His wedding ring.

The heat pounding through her veins instantly cooled. She eased her mouth from his and drew in a slow, deep breath.

She knew that he was no longer married. Not technically. But the fact that he still wore the ring confirmed that he still felt connected—and committed—to the woman he'd married. Until he was ready to take that ring off his finger, it would a mistake for Rachel to think that a relationship between them could lead to anything other than heartache.

With genuine regret, she pulled her hand from his. As her fingers curled around the knob of the door, she held his gaze for another moment, wishing the evening could be ending differently.

"Good night, Andrew."

Chapter Five

As Andrew drove back to his empty house, he found himself thinking about—and regretting—Rachel's abrupt withdrawal.

He knew why she'd pulled back when he'd decided he was ready to move full speed ahead. It was the wedding ring he'd almost forgotten was still on his finger.

The gold band had been there for so long that he honestly didn't even think about it anymore. Nor had he ever given serious consideration to taking it off. For a long time after his wife had died, he'd refused to even contemplate relinquishing this reminder of the vows they'd made to one another. He'd removed Nina's engagement ring and wedding band from her finger before the funeral, and he'd put them aside for Maura one day, but there had been no reason to take off his own.

Because he'd still felt married. He certainly didn't love his wife any less just because she wasn't there anymore.

In fact, for months he'd continued to sleep on "his"

side of the bed, and woken up in the morning reaching for her. And when he'd remembered that she wasn't there, his heart had ached. Gradually the pain had faded, but still the gold band had remained. As he twisted the ring around his finger now, he wondered if it was time for that to change.

No one had ever seemed to worry about its significance before. Certainly it hadn't prevented other women from propositioning him. He wondered what it said about Rachel that she couldn't ignore this symbol of his commitment to someone else.

If they ended up in bed together, would it mean more to her than just sex? Was she looking for a relationship? What was the rationale behind her sixteen-month dating hiatus? Because he was sure there had to be a reason.

Was she looking for a casual relationship or something a little more serious? She was only twenty-seven years old—the same age as his youngest brother, and the same age he'd been when he'd married Nina, two years his junior. And although that had only been eight years ago, he knew that a lot of women today didn't want to think about settling down until they were in their thirties, if even then.

Was Rachel one of those women? Did she ever want to marry and have kids? And why was he even asking himself these questions after two dates? Or was it only one date? Their Valentine's Day encounter, when they'd had dinner together at Valentino's and then gone bowling, probably didn't even count as a date. It had simply been a spontaneous outing of two people who didn't have any other plans.

But the fact was, he'd found himself thinking about her a lot since that night—even when he'd deliberately tried to put her out of his mind.

Nate would say that he was horny, and no doubt that was a factor. He hadn't been with a woman since Nina, and she'd been gone more than three years now.

He'd been attracted to other women, had felt the stirring of desire in his blood. But that stirring had never been strong enough to spur him into action. He'd kissed other women, but none of those kisses had made him want more. Now that he'd kissed Rachel, he actually ached with wanting.

Maybe it was finally time to take off his ring and look to his future rather than hold on to the past.

As a result of owning and operating Buy The Book—a local bookstore—for more than fifty years, Phoebe Lamontagne knew a lot of people in Charisma. The explosion of online publishing and selling had put a lot of bricks-and-mortar bookstores out of business, but Buy The Book not only remained standing, it continued to be successful. A few years earlier, Phoebe had brought in her youngest granddaughter, Kinsley, as a partner in the business so that she could retire. But every day that the shop opened its doors, Phoebe was there.

Most people agreed that it had to be difficult for her to let go of something that had been part of her usual routine for more than fifty years, and a lot of the store's regular customers looked forward to chatting with her as they browsed the shelves and made their purchases. It was only her most loyal customers and closest friends who had been invited to have tea in the back, where Phoebe dealt tarot cards and performed palm readings.

Rachel and Holly had spent a lot of time in that back room with Phoebe when they were kids. They'd been fascinated by the crystals and the charms and the scents and colors. As they grew older and began to understand more about the nature of the business, Holly had taken a deliberate step back, not wanting to be involved with what she referred to as her grandmother's hocus-pocus. Rachel had considered it a harmless hobby, and although she'd missed lazy afternoons hanging out in the back room, she'd stuck with her best friend.

As she weaved her way through the crowd that had gathered in the store to celebrate Phoebe's birthday, Rachel smiled to realize that most of those in attendance had been in Phoebe's magic room at various times throughout the years. She found the nonagenarian in the storytime circle of the kids' department, blatantly flirting with Calvin Russell, a recently divorced chiropractor who was at least forty years her junior.

"Sorry to interrupt, Gram," Rachel said, kissing the old woman's cheek.

"Calvin and I were just discussing some new adjustments that might help me sleep better," Phoebe told her.

"And I was monopolizing the guest of honor," the doctor realized. "Call me this week, Phoebs, and we'll set something up."

"I will," she promised.

He left with a "Happy Birthday" and a kiss on the old woman's cheek.

Rachel waited until Calvin was out of hearing before she asked, "Since when do you have trouble sleeping, *Phoebs?*"

"Since never," Phoebe admitted.

"So why do you need to see a chiropractor?"

"Because it's only one of a very few ways that a woman my age gets to feel a man's hands on her body."

The comment was so typically Phoebe, Rachel couldn't help but laugh. "I hope you live another ninety years," she said sincerely.

Gram smiled. "I'm glad you came today. I know you're busy with the shop, and it means a lot to me that you're here."

"I wouldn't be anywhere else," she said, and offered the square package she'd brought. "Happy Birthday."

The old woman ran her hands over the box, assessing its size and shape. "It's from The Sweet Spot," she decided. "Something truly decadent and delicious... Maybe Belgian chocolate truffles."

"If you could tell that much through the paper, you must be psychic."

Phoebe chuckled and patted the empty seat beside her, urging Rachel to sit. "Or I have faith that you remembered my favorite indulgence."

"Always," Rachel promised.

"So why are you here by yourself?"

"I'm not—I came with Holly."

Gram shook her head. "I meant, why didn't you bring your boyfriend?"

"I don't have one," Rachel told her, because as much as she might wish otherwise, she didn't think two impromptu outings and a couple of sizzling kisses made Andrew Garrett her boyfriend.

"Why not?"

"I'm too busy enjoying the single life," she said lightly.

Phoebe shook her head. "That's always Holly's excuse, and I'm afraid, in her case, it's true. She doesn't like to be tied down—or she thinks she doesn't, because she worries that she's got wanderlust in her veins like her mother. But you want roots, stability, a family."

"I thought you retired from all aspects of your business."

"Some signs are too obvious to ignore."

"What signs?" Rachel challenged.

"The wistful expression on your face when you saw Stuart Torrance touch his pregnant wife's belly."

Her smile was wry. "Okay, you caught me."

"So I'll ask you again—why don't you have a boyfriend?"

"I seem to be attracted to all the wrong men."

The older woman's gaze narrowed. "You're holding something back."

"It's your birthday, Gram. You should be mingling with your family and friends, not trying to solve my relationship woes."

"I wish I could steer you toward my grandson, Gary, but he's not the right man for you."

"Why not?" she asked curiously.

"He's too much like his sister. You need someone who wants the same thing you do—roots, family, commitment. But also someone who fires your passion and pushes you beyond your comfort zone." She looked into Rachel's eyes, and her lips curved. "You've already met him, haven't you?"

Though she was a little unnerved by the woman's apparent insights, she forced herself to respond lightly. "You're the fortune-teller, you tell me."

"You've already met him," Phoebe said again, and it wasn't a question this time. "But you're still trying to figure out if he's the one."

"Is he?"

The old woman shook her head. "That's not for me to say—only you can decide."

"Can't you at least give me a hint? Warn me if he's going to break my heart?"

"All I can tell you is that nothing worthwhile comes easily." Phoebe laid her hands, wrinkled but strong, on top of Rachel's. "You have a good heart. Don't be afraid to follow it."

Holly crossed the room to where they were seated and quickly assessed the situation. "No hocus-pocus on your birthday, Gram."

"It's not hocus-pocus."

"What it is, is time for cake," her granddaughter said, in an attempt to ward off a familiar confrontation.

"You better not have put ninety candles on that cake, or we're going to need the fire department."

"I should have thought of that," Holly lamented. "It would have been a great way to meet some sexy firefighters."

Her grandmother swatted at her. "You need to focus less on sexy and more on stability."

"I'm twenty-eight years old—I've got my whole life ahead of me for stability. Right now I want sexy."

"What kind of cake?" Rachel asked, trying to steer them both to a safer topic of conversation.

"Vanilla sponge with lemon filling and buttercream icing."

"Did you make it?" Gram asked.

"I was in charge of flowers," Holly reminded her. "Charlotte did the cake."

"Then it should be edible."

"Hey," Holly protested the subtle dig while Rachel tried not to smile. Her friend's ineptitude in the kitchen was legendary.

Phoebe smiled as she tucked her hand in her granddaughter's. "Did I mention how absolutely gorgeous the flowers are?"

Over the past couple of years, it had become part of the routine for Andrew and Maura to stay for dinner with her grandparents when he picked his daughter up at the end of a weekend visit. Andrew had never felt uncomfortable during these meals. Then again, he'd never before had his mind preoccupied by thoughts of any woman but their daughter while he was at their table.

Until tonight.

Tonight, as he poured gravy on his pork roast, it was Rachel who was on his mind. And as much as he tried to focus on Ed and Carol's conversation about their recent bridge tournament, his thoughts continued to wander.

"Andrew."

He glanced up to find his former father-in-law looking at him expectantly.

"Sorry?"

"I asked if you wouldn't mind passing the gravy," Ed said.

"Of course," he agreed, looking around the table for it—only to realize the pitcher was still in his hand.

When the meal was finally finished and he had Maura's overnight bag in hand, Carol handed him an envelope.

"What's this?"

"A birthday party invitation for Maura."

"Oh, right," his daughter said excitedly. "It's Jolene's birthday next week."

It took him a minute to remember that Jolene was the granddaughter of the Leighton's housekeeper. The Leightons lived directly behind the Wakefields, and Maura and Jolene had met the previous summer when Maura kicked a ball over the fence and into the Leightons' backyard.

Carol had tried to discourage the friendship, making no secret of the fact that she disapproved of her granddaughter fraternizing with the help. But Jolene was a sweet girl, and every time Maura went to visit her grandparents, she wanted to visit Jolene, too.

"Can I come to the party, Daddy?"

"We'll check our schedule when we get home," he promised.

"Maura can stay here again next weekend, if that makes it easier for you," Carol told him.

Andrew immediately shook his head. While he appreciated the offer, he knew it wasn't actually intended to make anything easier for him but to finagle some extra time with her granddaughter. She probably didn't even want Maura to go to the party except that it served her own purposes.

"Thanks," he said. "But we'll figure something out."

When they got home, they packed Maura's lunch for school the next day, then she had her bath and put on her pajamas. After her teeth were brushed, they snuggled together on her bed to read for a while. When the chapter was finished, he tucked her under the covers, gave her a hug and a kiss and turned out the light.

He cherished every minute of every day that he had with his little girl, but he still felt lonely sometimes. Restless and unsettled, he went to the cabinet behind his desk and poured himself a glass of scotch. He settled into the soft leather chair with his drink and sipped the rich amber liquid, enjoying the familiar burn as it slid down his throat.

He missed having someone to talk to at the end of the day, missed falling asleep with someone beside him and waking up with that same someone the next morning. As he realized the direction his thoughts had taken, he knew that his doubts and concerns about his readiness to move forward with his life were unfounded.

Not so very long ago he would have said that he missed talking to *Nina,* falling asleep beside *her* and waking up with *her.* Not so very long ago, he couldn't have imagined that "someone" being anyone else. Now when he thought of "someone" it was Rachel's face that came to mind, the image of her smile that filled his heart, the memory of her laughter that made him smile.

The sound of light footsteps on the stairs drew him out of his reverie just before Maura poked her head inside the doorway. He set his drink aside as she padded across the floor, then she crawled into his lap and he wrapped his arm around her to cuddle her close. She used to sit in his lap all the time when she was younger, claiming it was her favorite chair in the whole world. That had changed in preschool. A lot of things had changed in preschool.

His lips curved as he breathed in the scent of her shampoo. She might be growing up, but she still smelled like his little girl.

"Why are you out of bed?" he asked, more curiosity than censure in his tone.

"I forgot to tell you something."

"What's that?"

"Mrs. Patterson wrote a note in my agenda for you."

He held back a sigh. "Mrs." Patterson was actually "Ms." Patterson, as she'd made a point of clarifying when he'd met her at the beginning of the year. Her divorce had been final for almost two years and her only regret was that she and her husband never had any children. She absolutely loved children—that was, after all, the reason she'd decided to become a teacher. And his daughter, Mara, was simply a joy to have in her classroom.

"Maura," he'd said, automatically corrected her on the pronunciation. She'd flushed in acknowledgment of her mistake but forged ahead, gushing about Maura's sweet nature and quick mind.

Their second meeting had taken place under very different circumstances, when Andrew went to the school in response to a call from the principal after Maura had given one of her classmates a bloody nose. After listening to the principal's spiel about his daughter's inappropriate behavior, Mrs. Patterson had taken a different tack.

The teacher assured him that she empathized with how difficult it must be for the single father of a little girl, and she'd suggested that he should ensure that Maura had appropriate female influences in her life. The subtext was clear, and Andrew had politely—but quickly—extricated himself from the situation.

"Have you been beating up Tyler Buckle again?" he asked his daughter now.

"I didn't beat him up," she denied, with a put-upon sigh. "I punched him—once. And he deserved it."

"It doesn't matter if you think he deserved it." Although privately, Andrew had agreed with her—and had been impressed by the impact of her right hook. "You don't solve disagreements with violence."

"He called me an orphan," she reminded him.

"Which only proves that he doesn't know the definition of the word."

"But I don't have a mommy…and I don't even remember her very much anymore."

"I know, honey." And that knowledge made his heart ache. Although he'd made sure to keep photos of Nina around the house, those pictures were a poor substitute for the real thing.

"Do you think I'll ever get a new mommy?"

He probably should have anticipated the question after she'd come home from school a couple of weeks earlier with the news that her friend, Kristy, was getting a new daddy. And though he'd held his breath for a moment, when she'd said nothing else about it then, he'd thought the subject was done. He should have known better. Maura had a habit of hitting him with the hard questions when he least expected them—and this one was harder than any other question she'd ever asked.

"I don't know," he finally said. "It's not as if you can pick one out as easily as you would a carton of ice cream at the grocery store."

"I know," she agreed. "You hafta find a girl you think is pretty and marry her."

He smiled at the simplistic explanation. "*Pretty* is good."

"Do you think Mrs. Patterson is pretty?"

He tried to picture his daughter's teacher, but it was Rachel's image that filled his mind. Her hair was brown, but it was a blend of so many shades, dark and light, and silky to the touch. Her eyes were deep blue and sparkled with life, and the sweet curve of her soft mouth was irresistibly tempting.

"Not as pretty as Rachel."

"Who's Rachel?"

He hadn't meant to speak the thought aloud. He certainly hadn't intended to mention Rachel to his daughter, but he'd been thinking about her so often that her name just slipped out. "Just someone I know."

"Do I know her?"

He shook his head.

"Are you gonna marry her?"

"There are a lot of things that have to happen before a boy and a girl marry."

She nodded, obviously wise beyond her years. "You hafta go out on some dates and kiss her first, and then you get married."

"How do you know all this stuff?" he asked.

"Kristy Sutherland. Her mom used to go on lotsa dates and kiss lotsa boys."

"Kristy told you this?"

Maura nodded again. "Did you go on a date with Rachel?"

"We went to a basketball game yesterday, when you were at Grandma and Grandpa's," he admitted.

"Did you kiss her?"

"I'm not sure this is an appropriate conversation to be having with my six-year-old daughter," he said.

"I'm almost seven," she reminded him.

"It's still not appropriate."

"You kissed her," Maura decided.

He sighed. "I think it's time to get you back into bed, Little Miss Nosy Pants."

She giggled at the nickname, and the sound squeezed his heart. Her recollection of Nina was fading, and he wished there was something he could say or do to help her hold on to the few memories that she had. On the other hand, she'd been absolutely inconsolable when she'd learned her mother wasn't ever coming home again. She'd cried and cried and cried, and when absolute and complete exhaustion had finally forced her to sleep, she'd been restless even in slumber.

Andrew hadn't wanted to take her to the funeral. He'd wanted her to remember Nina as she'd been when she was alive—full of life and laughter. The minister had suggested to Andrew that Maura needed to be there, to see her mother at rest and say a final goodbye. So he'd relented—and had sorely regretted it.

As if the loss of her mother wasn't difficult enough, Maura had been further traumatized by the sight of her still body and pale visage in the casket. She'd shaken her head, stubbornly refusing to believe that woman was her mother. "Mommy smiles and laughs and her eyes are bright and she puts her arms around me when I'm sad."

Andrew had been certain that his heart was completely shattered over the loss of the woman he'd loved, but Maura's inconsolable grief had ground those jagged little pieces into dust.

It had been a long time after that before he'd even managed to coax a smile out of his little girl, and longer still before she laughed again. The childish giggle was no longer as infrequent as it had been in that first year after Nina's death, but the joyful sound still tugged at his heart. If Maura's question about getting a new mother wasn't proof enough, that giggle reinforced his certainty that she was happy again.

Maybe it was time for him to be happy, too.

He lowered her onto the mattress and tucked the covers up around her. "Sweet dreams, baby."

Her eyes, already drifting shut, popped open again. "When am I going to meet her?"

"Meet who?"

Her brow furrowed as she struggled to remember the name he hadn't intended to mention. "Rachel?"

"Rachel who?"

"That's not fair—you never told me her last name."

"Whose last name?"

She giggled again. "Daddy," she admonished.

He kissed her forehead. "I love you, baby."

"I love you, too, Daddy."

As he made his way back downstairs, he thought about Maura's request to meet Rachel. He'd never been tempted to introduce any other woman to his daughter, but this time was different. Rachel was different. She was a woman who meant far more to him than he would have expected after only two dates, and he wanted her to meet the little girl who meant more to him than anything else in the world.

But first he had to find that note in Maura's agenda.

He frowned as he read the handwritten message from Denise Patterson, asking him to call and including her home telephone number. Immediately concerned, he did so. Twenty minutes later, he was reassured and more than a little annoyed.

Apparently all she wanted to talk about was a flyer she'd sent home the previous week to promote an after-school drama program that she thought would help Maura overcome her shyness. He didn't think his daughter was any more introverted than most little girls her age, but he thanked Ms. Patterson for her concern and ended the conversation as quickly as possible.

Then, because he had the phone in his hand, he took a business card out of his wallet and dialed a different number.

Chapter Six

When Andrew said that he would call, Rachel believed him. He didn't seem like the kind of guy to play games, so she figured she'd hear from him by the middle of the week. It didn't occur to her, when the phone rang just after nine o'clock Sunday night, that it might be him.

When she saw his name on the display, her heart started pounding hard and fast. And when she reached for the receiver, she felt like a schoolgirl with a crush on the cutest boy in the class. Except that Andrew Garrett definitely wasn't a boy, and the fantasies that had played out in her dreams the night before weren't anything like the innocent fantasies of her youth.

"You sound surprised to hear from me," he said, after they'd exchanged basic pleasantries.

"I am," she admitted. "I know you said you'd call, but I thought that meant sometime during the week." Certainly most of the guys she knew would have waited rather than risk appearing too eager.

"Is it okay that I called? Or do you now think I'm pathetically desperate?"

"It's more than okay," she assured him. "I don't think you're either pathetic or desperate." In fact, she was pleased by this proof that he'd been thinking about her, too. Probably not as often or as obsessively as she'd been thinking about him, but still.

"And would it be okay if I took you out for lunch tomorrow?" he asked.

"Definitely."

"What time?"

She wanted to say 8:00 a.m. so that she didn't have to wait too long to see him again, but that might be a little bit early for lunch. Maybe she should propose breakfast instead—preferably after they rolled out of her bed together. Of course, she didn't suggest either of those things.

Instead, she said, "Mondays are usually slow, so I can probably get away around one."

"I'll see you then," he promised.

She was already looking forward to it.

And when she woke up the next morning, her lunch date with Andrew was the first thought on her mind. As she dressed for the day, she took a little more care than usual with her appearance. She opted for a pair of slim-fitting charcoal trousers with a slight flare at the bottom and topped them with a long-sleeved dove-gray sweater, then added chunky silver hoops to her ears and slipped a trio of bangle bracelets onto her wrist. A swipe of eyeliner, a touch of mascara, a dab of lip gloss, and she was ready. A final glance in the mirror assured her that she looked stylish but not overdone.

And then she got into the shop and learned—via the numerous orders for funeral wreaths and bereavement baskets—that Nigel Hanson had died.

Nigel and Harriet Hanson lived in South Ridge, but

their youngest son, Curtis, had gone to school with Rachel and Holly. It was a tentative connection but enough that when Buds & Blooms opened, Nigel brought his business to them.

In addition to the usual requests for his wife's birthday, their anniversary and arrangements to celebrate the birth of each of their five grandchildren, Nigel had a standing order for a single yellow rose delivered on the third day of every month to celebrate the anniversary of the day he and Harriet first met. Rachel knew that his wife of fifty-five years would be devastated by his passing.

She and Holly were so busy making arrangements for delivery to the funeral home that Rachel completely lost track of time—and even forgot about her lunch date—until Andrew walked into the shop.

She looked at him, then at the clock, then winced. "I'm so sorry."

"You forgot?"

"Lost track of time," she admitted, and briefly explained about Mr. Hanson.

"It's okay," he told her. "I know what it's like to be at the wrong end of a business emergency."

The statement surprised her. He hadn't gone into much detail about his work, but what he had told her about carpentry didn't indicate that it was the type of work that experienced many emergencies.

But before she could follow up on his comment, he said, "Have you eaten?"

She shook her head. "No, but there's no way I can get away right now."

"I'm not asking you to—I'm asking if you want ham, turkey or roast beef?"

She realized he was offering to pick up sandwiches from The Corner Deli across the street, proving that he was both flexible and generous, and she was sincerely touched by his offer. "I feel like I should say 'no thanks' but I'm going to say 'turkey' instead."

"What about Holly?" he asked.

"Roast beef," she called out, confirming her presence in the back room and that she'd been shamelessly eavesdropping on their conversation.

"One turkey, one roast beef," Andrew confirmed, then pressed a quick kiss to Rachel's lips. "I'll be back in ten."

It was closer to fifteen minutes before he returned with a take-out bag from The Corner Deli in hand. In addition to the sandwiches, he'd ordered potato wedges and coleslaw and cold drinks. He'd even had the foresight to ask for paper plates and cutlery, and he set everything out on one of the smaller worktables while Rachel and Holly washed up.

"Thank you," Holly said sincerely. "I was so hungry I was ready to start gnawing on discarded stems."

"A different spin on the traditional plant-based diet," Andrew mused.

Holly chuckled, and Rachel was smiling as she unwrapped her sandwich, pleased to witness the easy banter between Andrew and her friend. He sat down beside Rachel and scooped some potato wedges onto his plate to go with his turkey sandwich.

There were the usual interruptions while they ate—phones to be answered and walk-in customers to be served—and in between they chatted a little about Phoebe's birthday party the day before and the sideboard Andrew was working on and the new guy Holly had met when she picked her brother up at the airport Saturday afternoon.

"I enjoyed that," Rachel said, folding her napkin. "Although I'm sure it wasn't what you had in mind when you invited me to lunch today."

"It wasn't," Andrew agreed. "But at least I got to see you—even if it was through a veil of flowers."

Holly finished her lunch then picked up her empty plate and cup to dump them in the garbage. "I'm going to stretch my legs," she told them, and headed toward the front of the store.

"I think she was trying to give us some privacy."

"Very considerate of her," Andrew said, taking Rachel's hand to tug her off her stool and into his arms.

"I've got cuttings and leaves all over me," she protested.

"I don't care," he said, and lowered his mouth to hers.

It wasn't as passionate as the kisses they'd shared Saturday night—which was probably a good thing, considering the time and place—but there was still enough heat that she all but melted against him.

"You're really good at that," she murmured, when he eased his mouth from hers.

His lips curved. "You inspire me."

"I have to get back to work," she said, with obvious reluctance.

"Me, too," he told her. "But there was something I wanted to tell you—"

"Another two orders just came in," Holly said, returning to the workroom and heading directly to the refrigerated storage to gather the necessary flowers.

Rachel kept her focus on Andrew, her curiosity piqued more by the seriousness of his expression than the words. "What is it?"

But he shook his head. "It can wait."

"You're sure."

"Positive." He touched his lips to hers again. "I'll call you."

"Tonight?" she asked hopefully.

"Tonight."

"Obviously things went well on Saturday," Holly commented when Andrew had gone.

"It was close, but the Wolfpack emerged victorious," Rachel said.

Her friend rolled her eyes. "I wasn't asking about the game."

"You know I'm not the type to kiss and tell."

"Yes, you are—at least to your best friend."

Rachel laughed, because it was true. "You probably have more to tell than I do."

Holly smiled. "That depends on whether or not you can top five orgasms."

Rachel's jaw dropped. "You met this guy on Saturday and you slept with him already?"

"Actually, there was no sleeping involved."

"None?"

"I got a few hours after I sent him home."

"You had sex with him and then kicked him out of your apartment?"

"I like my space," Holly said, just a little defensively.

"You like sex without intimacy."

"Thanks for that dime-store analysis."

She sighed. "You're never going to find the right guy when you keep looking in all the wrong places."

"And you're so busy looking for the perfect guy that you overlook a lot of really great ones."

Rachel frowned, wondering if there might not be some truth in what her friend was saying.

"Andrew is a prime example," Holly insisted.

"A prime example of what?"

"The prime male. He's tall, dark and incredibly sexy. His shoulders are broad enough that a woman would feel confident that she could lean on him, his arms are strong enough that she would feel safe in his embrace, and he looks as if he walked off the cover of a men's magazine. But most importantly—he's single."

"Widowed," Rachel clarified, not sure if she should be

impressed or annoyed at the observation skills that had allowed her friend to so accurately catalog his physical attributes. "And you were the one who warned me not to rush into anything—that a man who still buys flowers for a wife who's been gone more than three years is probably still in love with her."

"I did say that," Holly acknowledged. "I changed my mind."

"On the basis of what?"

"The way he looked at you."

"How did he look at me?"

"Like he was picturing you naked."

"He almost had me naked Saturday night," Rachel admitted.

"Seriously?"

She nodded. "One kiss, and I felt as if my clothes were going to melt off my body."

She still didn't know if Andrew was the right guy, but he certainly knew how to push all the right buttons. It had been more than sixteen months since she'd decided to take a break from dating. And in all that time, she hadn't thought too much about sex. Certainly she hadn't lamented the fact that she wasn't having any.

One kiss from Andrew Garrett and she was thinking about it a lot. Not sex in general but sex with him in particular. If he was half as good a lover as he was a kisser, he would be spectacular.

"So why'd you put the brakes on?" her friend wanted to know.

"Why are you so sure that it was me?"

"Because I saw the way he looked at you," Holly said again.

"Okay, it was me," she admitted. "Because I couldn't imagine getting naked with a guy who was still wearing the ring put on his finger by another woman."

Holly nodded. "I can understand that. But I saw something else today when he looked at you."

"What's that?"

"He isn't wearing his wedding ring anymore."

Andrew didn't expect the absence of the gold band on his finger would go completely unnoticed, but he was surprised that his youngest brother was the first to comment on it.

Shortly after he got back from lunch with Rachel, Daniel stopped by the office in which Andrew felt compelled to spend at least a few hours every day.

"What brings you into the hallowed halls of Garrett Furniture?" he asked his brother, because it was a well-known fact that Daniel preferred to keep as much distance as possible between himself and the family business.

"I need a favor."

Though there wasn't anything he wouldn't do for either of his brothers, experience cautioned him to ask, "What kind of favor?"

"I'm going to ask Mom and Dad to release my trust fund."

Before their maternal grandfather, Randall Willson, passed away more than a decade earlier, he'd set up trusts for each of his three grandsons. By his own admission, Randall had been a reckless and foolish young man. As a result, he'd decided that instead of the money being released when the beneficiary reached the age of twenty-one or even twenty-five, it should be held until the beneficiary was thirty—or legally married.

"Okay," Andrew said cautiously.

"I'm not asking you to support my request—I'm just asking you not to oppose it."

"Why would I oppose it?"

"I hope you won't," Daniel said again. "Because I want to invest in the ownership of a stock-car racing team."

The announcement didn't really surprise Andrew. His brother had always loved racing, and he'd made more than a few comments over the years expressing interest in getting involved in the business. But this time, it sounded as if he had a solid plan.

"I have no objection to whatever you want to do," Andrew assured him. "And even if I did, I doubt my opinion would factor into Mom and Dad's decision."

"You think they'll say no," Daniel guessed.

"I think, when you tell them what you want the money for, they'll shut you down faster than a red flag," he admitted.

"What if I start out talking about their fortieth anniversary party?"

"Have you started making plans for it?"

"Not exactly," his brother hedged.

"Then I wouldn't open with that," Andrew warned.

"This isn't fair," Daniel grumbled. "I'm twenty-seven years old, and I have to ask my parents for money."

Andrew wasn't unsympathetic. His brother had always wanted to do his own thing, make his own way. He'd deliberately chosen a career path separate from Garrett Furniture. He lived on his own and supported himself, but there was no way he made enough money to buy a racing team.

"What did Nate say about this?"

"He said that he would consider throwing in from his own trust fund if Mom and Dad turned me down."

Andrew considered that for a minute. "I could probably do the same, if I liked your business plan. Although I've already tied up half of my trust in a new fund for Maura."

"I'll keep that in mind as an absolute last resort, but I was really hoping to do this on my own."

On his own—but with money given to him by his

grandfather. Andrew wondered if his brother even recognized the inherent contradiction in the statement.

"You know, if Mom and Dad say no, there's always the marriage provision," he teased.

Daniel shuddered at the thought. "I don't think so."

Andrew pushed away from his desk and went to refill his coffee mug. He gestured to the pot. "Do you want a cup?"

His brother shook his head, then his gaze narrowed on the hand that was wrapped around the mug. "You're not wearing your wedding ring."

"I'm not married anymore."

"You haven't been married for three years," Daniel pointed out, not unkindly.

He nodded in acknowledgment of the fact. "I wasn't ready to take it off before now."

"So who is she?"

He could pretend not to know what his brother was talking about, but what was the point? "Her name's Rachel."

"Is she the one you went bowling with on Valentine's Day?"

"Honestly, you and Nate gossip about my love life like a couple of high school girls."

Daniel snorted. "You don't have a love life. Or has that changed?"

"I'm hoping to change it."

His brother considered, nodded. "Good for you."

"Really? That's it—no other snide remarks?"

"Nope. I'm happy for you."

"It's early stages yet," he said, cautioning himself as much as his brother.

"Does Maura like her?"

"I'm sure she will."

Daniel's brows winged up. "She hasn't met her yet?"

"No."

"Why not?"

"Because I haven't actually had a chance to tell Rachel about Maura."

"You've been dating this woman since Valentine's Day and she doesn't know you have a child?"

"We haven't been dating since Valentine's Day."

His brother frowned. "So this is someone else?"

"No. Rachel is the one I went out with on Valentine's Day, but I didn't see her again after that until this past weekend."

"And while you were with her this past weekend, you didn't manage to slip something into the conversation along the lines of 'by the way, I have a daughter'?"

"No, I didn't."

Daniel shook his head. "Man, even I know that's a recipe for disaster."

"I was planning to tell her at lunch today."

"Obviously that didn't happen."

"Our plans got changed," he said, aware that he sounded more than a little defensive.

"When this comes back to bite you in the ass, don't say I didn't warn you."

Andrew did call Rachel Monday night, and then again the next night, and the night after that. She enjoyed talking to him on the phone. She hadn't realized how rarely she had a telephone conversation that lasted more than a few minutes with anyone, even her family. It seemed like everyone preferred to communicate via text message or email these days.

Most of the time, Rachel appreciated the benefits of electronic communication, especially the convenience of sending or responding to messages on her own time. But she could easily listen to Andrew's voice for hours.

And even when she wasn't talking to him, she was

thinking about him—and thinking about the kisses they'd shared. And she couldn't help wondering what she'd be thinking about if they hadn't stopped after those few kisses.

It was easy enough to imagine the feel of his hands on her, the weight of his body pressing down on hers. But she didn't want to imagine; she wanted to know. And she felt like a hypocrite that she'd chastised Holly for sleeping with a man she barely knew when she was thinking about doing the same.

Unfortunately, she didn't see that happening anytime soon, especially when they couldn't seem to coordinate their schedules to get together again during the week. He was available Wednesday night, but she had a book-club meeting. She would have happily skipped the meeting to see him, except that she was hosting this month. She suggested they might be able to get together on Thursday, but he had already committed to helping his brother with something.

"Do you like art?" she asked, when he called her after her book club on Wednesday.

"It depends on who's defining the term *art*."

"I think, in this case, it refers to metal sculpture."

"That could have potential," he allowed.

"Elaine, one of our part-time employees, has an exhibit opening at the art gallery this weekend. I figured I should go check it out and be supportive, and I thought, if you didn't have any other plans, you might want to go with me."

"When?"

"Saturday afternoon."

"I'm sorry," he said, sounding genuinely regretful. "But I can't make it."

She was undeniably disappointed—and curious as to the reason behind his refusal. It didn't bother her that he had other plans, as he apparently did, but she wondered why he seemed unwilling to disclose what those plans were.

"Maybe we could get together Sunday afternoon," he suggested.

She and Holly tried to set a schedule so that they each got one weekend day off, but this week, Rachel's day off was Saturday. "I'm scheduled to work on Sunday."

"I wish I could switch my Saturday plans, but I can't."

"I might be able to get Trish to fill in for me at the shop," Rachel offered. "She's usually happy to get extra hours."

When he called her Thursday night after what he described as an unsuccessful meeting with his brother, she confirmed that she'd made the arrangements with Trish, and he said that he would pick her up at noon on Sunday.

She went to the art gallery on Saturday as planned, then she met Holly at the movie theater. It was the opening weekend for the film they'd chosen to see and the theater was rapidly filling up, so they went to find their seats before worrying about snacks. Since Holly had bought the tickets, Rachel left her to hold their seats while she went to get popcorn.

She was on her way to the concession stand when she saw him. "Andrew, hi."

He looked equally startled to see her—and not entirely pleased. "I thought you had something at the art gallery today."

"I did," she confirmed. "And I'm glad you didn't let me drag you along. Elaine is great with flowers, but I don't think the lumps of metal she put on display would fit anyone's definition of art."

He smiled, but it seemed forced, as if he wasn't really listening to what she was saying. It was then that she realized he was standing directly outside the entrance to the ladies' room, as if waiting for someone.

Probably the same someone with whom he was going to share the large popcorn and two drinks he carried.

"Oh." As all the pieces clicked into place in her mind, hot color filled her cheeks. "I'm sorry. I didn't realize…"

She trailed off, hurt and embarrassed and frustrated with herself for apologizing to him. Why was *she* sorry? She wasn't the one who had made some lame excuse about having plans in order to spend the afternoon with someone else.

He frowned. "What didn't you realize?"

Her cheeks burned hotter, but combined with the humiliation was anger that he would make her spell it out. "Obviously you're here on a date."

He was shaking his head before the words were completely out of her mouth. "No. I'm not."

But she didn't want to hear his denials. She didn't want to know how close she'd been to falling for yet another man who didn't know how to be honest.

"Enjoy your movie," she said, and started to move past him to the concession stand.

"Rachel, wait—" Andrew began.

But she'd already turned away and, in her haste, nearly bumped into the child who had exited the ladies' room and was moving toward him.

Then she heard the little girl say, "I'm ready now, Daddy."

Chapter Seven

Daddy?

Rachel froze, her shocked gaze moving from Andrew to the little girl and back again.

Was it possible that she'd misunderstood the child's words? But no, she could see it now. The familial resemblance wasn't obvious, but it was there—in the shape of her eyes, the curve of her mouth, and even the way she tilted her head when she looked at Rachel.

She was a beautiful girl with cornflower-blue eyes, a light dusting of freckles over the bridge of her nose, and a cupid's-bow mouth. Her shoulder-length blond hair was held away from her face with butterfly barrettes. The puffy purple coat she wore was unzipped to reveal a lilac-colored fleece sweater with a bouquet of pink applique daisies on the front and pink corduroy pants. If she had to guess, Rachel would say she was around seven years old, but all of the details that buzzed around in her mind were insignificant compared to the fact that this child was undoubtedly Andrew's child.

"This is my daughter, Maura," he confirmed. Then, to the little girl, "Maura, this is Rachel."

The child's eyes widened and her mouth curved, as if she was both surprised and sincerely pleased to meet her. "Are you going to see the movie with us?" Maura asked her.

"No," Rachel and Andrew answered quickly and in unison.

Maura's smile faded and she looked to her father, as if for an explanation.

"I didn't know Rachel was planning to be here today," he said. "And I'm sure she's not here to see *The Pixie Princess*."

"I'm not," Rachel confirmed.

"Okay." The little girl accepted the explanation easily. "Maybe next time?"

Her hopeful tone piqued Rachel's curiosity.

"Maura," her father said sternly.

"Speaking of movies," Rachel said. "Holly's probably wondering where I disappeared to, so I should get back to my seat before mine starts."

Andrew looked as if he wanted to say something, but then he only nodded.

Rachel shifted her gaze back to the little girl and managed a smile. "It was nice to meet you, Maura."

"It was nice to meet you, too," the child echoed politely.

She'd only taken a few steps when she heard Maura speak again. "You were right, Daddy. She's really pretty."

The statement only added to Rachel's confusion. Was it possible that Andrew had mentioned her to his daughter? But why? And why had he never even hinted to Rachel about the existence of his child?

She stopped inside the doorway of the theater and tried to organize her scrambled thoughts, but she didn't understand any of this. Had he lied to her? Or just withheld information? And was the distinction even relevant? Obviously she didn't know anything about the man if he'd kept such a monumental secret from her.

Maybe it was her fault. Maybe she hadn't asked the right questions. The next time she met a guy, she was going to ask him point-blank: do you have any wives or kids I should know about?

She climbed the stairs toward the back of the theater and squeezed down the aisle toward Holly.

Her friend looked puzzled when Rachel dropped into the seat beside her. "Popcorn?"

She winced. "I'm sorry."

"You went to get popcorn…and you forgot the popcorn?"

"I ran into Andrew on my way to the concession stand." She shook her head. "No, not just Andrew. Andrew and his daughter."

Holly frowned. "I didn't know he had a kid."

"Neither did I."

"Oh."

Rachel nodded.

"I'm sorry, Rach."

She nodded again. She was sorry, too. Sorry and sad and angry. She'd honestly thought that he was different, that he was a good guy who might not trample all over her heart. She'd been wrong.

She drew in a deep breath and forced herself to push all thoughts of Andrew Garrett to the back of her mind. The previews were just starting, so she figured the line at the concession stand would be gone. "I'll go get our snacks now," she whispered to Holly.

But her friend shook her head. "Forget the popcorn. After the movie, we're going to Marg & Rita's."

* * *

Marg & Rita's was one of downtown Charisma's hidden gems. Tucked beside the library and in the shadow of the town hall, it wasn't obvious to someone who didn't know it was there. But anyone who lived or worked in the downtown core knew about it.

The restaurant was owned by two women—neither of them named Marg or Rita—and boasted authentic Mexican cuisine and more than twenty-five different flavors of margaritas.

The male waiter offered menus, but Rachel and Holly already knew what they wanted: a plate of nachos supreme and two traditional margaritas. Their beverages were delivered almost immediately, and Rachel lifted the glass to her lips to take a long sip of the tart icy drink.

"I've been thinking about this," Holly said, after she'd sampled her own margarita. "Maybe it's not as big a deal as you think."

"He has a child—I'm not sure any deal gets bigger than that."

"But you like kids," her friend reminded her.

"I do," she agreed. "The issue isn't his daughter...it's that he didn't tell me about his daughter."

"He told you he'd been married. You didn't think to ask if they had any kids?"

"No—I was too busy empathizing over the fact that his wife had died."

Holly winced. "Okay. I can see how that might have deflected any further inquiries."

The waiter delivered a heaping plate of crisp tortilla chips layered with spicy ground beef, onions, tomatoes and jalapeños, and covered in melted cheese.

"Thank God—I'm starving," Holly said.

"Or you could thank the waiter," Rachel suggested drily.

Her friend glanced up at the server and gave him a wide smile. "Thank you—sincerely."

"You're welcome." He returned the smile.

Rachel lifted her glass to her lips and realized it was empty.

"Can I bring you ladies another round?"

"Yes, please." One of the other great things about Marg & Rita's was that it was within easy walking distance of Rachel's apartment.

Holly dug into the plate of nachos with enthusiasm. Although it was one of Rachel's favorite menu items, too, she wasn't feeling very hungry tonight. But she put a couple of chips on her plate and nibbled on them.

"Getting back to the topic of our conversation," Holly said, and popped a jalapeño in her mouth. "I just think you should consider giving Andrew a chance to explain before you write him off completely."

"Okay." Rachel dunked a chip in sour cream. "Considered and discarded."

Her friend shook her head, but a smile was tugging at the corners of her mouth. "It's not like you to be so rigid and unforgiving."

"It's the new me—the one determined not to end up with her heart broken again."

"But you know there's got to be more to the story."

"And I'm not willing to get sucked in by another man's story," Rachel told her.

"Another... Oh. Eric."

She nodded.

Holly wrinkled her nose. "I forgot about him."

Rachel couldn't forget, and she wouldn't let herself make the same mistake again.

She'd started dating Eric a few years earlier. She'd met him at a housewarming party for some mutual friends and she'd fallen for him hard and fast. He'd been upfront with her from the beginning, admitting that he was recently divorced and shared custody of his eleven-year-old daughter, Summer.

Although she'd been eager to meet his child, they'd dated for six months before Eric had let that happen. Rachel understood his reticence, and she appreciated that he didn't want his daughter to get attached to someone who might not be around for the long haul. He was trying to protect her from the disappointment she experienced every time her mother—his ex-wife—broke up with yet another boyfriend. So when Eric finally introduced Rachel to Summer, she thought it meant that he wanted her to be a part of both of their lives.

But every time they had plans to do something together with his daughter, his ex-wife would interfere. It was a testament to how naive Rachel was that she didn't realize he was still in love with Wendy. Every time his ex-wife called, he would jump. He would cancel plans with Rachel without apology in order to hang a picture on Wendy's bedroom wall or perform some other menial task. Once, they'd been in the middle of sex and he'd answered a hysterical call about a mouse in Wendy's basement—and then he left Rachel naked in his bed to go dispose of the rodent.

Every holiday and birthday was a family celebration, which meant that Eric spent it with Summer and Wendy. Rachel had been willing to accept second place in his life—she understood that his daughter was his first priority, as she should be. But she'd sincerely resented that he was more considerate of his ex-wife's feelings than he was of her own.

"The situation with Andrew is completely different," Holly said now. "He doesn't have an ex-wife pulling his strings from behind the scenes."

"No," Rachel agreed. "But I think I understand better now why it was so difficult for him to take his wedding band off. Nina wasn't just his wife…she was the mother of his child."

"But he has taken it off," her friend reminded her.

"He still didn't tell me about his child."

Holly sighed. "I just think you should let him explain."

Rachel had no interest in his explanations. In fact, she wouldn't have minded if she never saw him or talked to him again.

But when she slipped her key in her lock and realized that her phone was ringing, she automatically raced across the room to answer it because it didn't occur to her tequila-clouded mind that it might be Andrew.

"Hello?"

"Hi."

He only said one word—barely one syllable—but she recognized his voice immediately. She sat down on the edge of the couch and willed her head to stop spinning so she could focus. "Why are you calling, Andrew?"

"I wanted to apologize."

"No apology necessary," she said coldly.

"I should have told you about Maura."

And she couldn't help thinking that he would have told her if he'd ever planned on introducing her to his child. The fact that he'd never mentioned the little girl's existence proved that Rachel didn't matter enough to him to share the details of his life. They'd gone out a couple of times and shared a few kisses, but he'd obviously never intended for their relationship to go any further than that.

"I handled the situation badly," he acknowledged. "I've never been in the position of having to introduce my daughter to a woman I was dating, because I haven't had more than one date with anyone since Nina died."

He sounded sincere, but she wasn't going to let herself get sucked in. "So what is the magic number? How many dates did we need to have before you decided to tell me that you had a child?"

"I wanted to tell you. I tried to tell you."

"When? Because I'm pretty sure if you'd said anything that even remotely hinted at the existence of a child, I would have remembered."

"Monday," he said. "The reason I wanted to have lunch with you on Monday was to tell you about Maura. But then you couldn't get away from the shop, and I didn't want to dump that kind of news on you when you were obviously distracted by other things."

Thinking back, she did remember that he'd started to say something before Holly had interrupted him. But how could she really know what he'd intended to say? How could she know he wasn't just making an excuse after the fact? And why hadn't he made any other attempt since?

"That was five days ago," she pointed out. "And we've talked on the phone every day."

"I wanted to tell you in person."

She was wavering, and she didn't want to waver. She wanted to stand firm and righteous and protect her heart. The more time she'd spent with Andrew, the more she'd realized that she could easily fall for the man, but that was a risk she was willing to take. Now she knew there was a lot more at stake.

The sexy man was a father and his little girl was too adorable to resist, and falling for both of them would definitely lead to heartache. And she'd been there and done that once before.

"Will you still have lunch with me tomorrow and give me a chance to grovel?"

She wasn't sure that was a good idea. She didn't want to get drawn deeper into his world and start to care for him, only to find out that he was just like Eric.

"Please," he added, when she didn't immediately respond.

The single word—or maybe it was the sincerity in his tone—tugged at her heartstrings.

"I'm only asking for an hour of your time," he continued. "If, after that hour, you don't want to see me again, I promise to respect your decision."

She wasn't worried about him—she was worried about herself. That she would be willing to take whatever crumbs he was offering her. When would she learn her lesson? When would she realize that she deserved to be with someone who was willing to make her a priority in his life?

"Will Maura be there?" she asked.

"No, she's going to a birthday party tomorrow."

If he'd said yes, she might have given him the benefit of the doubt. But it seemed more than convenient that he'd made plans with her when Maura would be somewhere else—it seemed contrived. He hadn't intended for her to know his daughter—that part of his life was off-limits. And no way was she going there again.

But she would have lunch with him tomorrow—so that she could tell him, face-to-face, that she wasn't going to get involved with him. She was going to end their relationship before it really had a chance to begin, before she fell for him more completely than she'd already done.

"Where did you want to go for lunch?"

"Why don't we decide after I pick you up?" he suggested.

"I'd rather meet you." That way, she could walk out when she was ready.

"Okay," he relented. "How about noon at Chez Henri?"

She frowned at the unfamiliar name. "Where's that?"

He rattled off an address on Evergreen Trail, which she realized could only be in Forrest Hill. No wonder she didn't recognize the name of the restaurant—she didn't spend a lot of time in that part of town. If Chez Henri had prices to fit its location, lunch was going to be an expensive meal.

She experienced a slight twinge of guilt that she was going to let him buy her lunch and then never see him again, until she reminded herself that she'd tried—several times—to decline his invitation but he'd been insistent.

The next day, Rachel followed his directions into a residential part of the exclusive neighborhood. It turned out that the address he'd given for Chez Henri wasn't a restaurant at all but a two-story Georgian-style home.

She might have thought she'd written the address down incorrectly except that she recognized his Infiniti in the driveway. That was when she suspected that he'd kept more secrets from her than the existence of his child. He'd said he was a carpenter, but the gorgeous home in this exclusive neighborhood suggested that he might be connected to a multimillion-dollar furniture company.

He hadn't been sure she would come. Despite her agreement, Andrew suspected that as soon as Rachel turned onto Evergreen Trail and realized there were no restaurants in sight, she might turn around again. But because he was watching through the window, he saw the lime-green Fiesta slow down in front of his house, then stop in the middle of the road.

He opened the front door and stepped outside, and after about half a minute, the car pulled into the driveway.

He walked down the flagstone path to meet her. Spring had finally started to show signs of its arrival, and the sight of the crocuses poking their heads up through the soil almost made him forget the frigid temperatures of a few weeks earlier. Then Rachel got out of her car, and he found an even-better reason to appreciate the warmer weather.

She was wearing a skirt. A softly flowing number in pale pink that swirled around her knees and drew his attention downward to deliciously slender calves and ankles. Over the skirt she wore a long-sleeved ivory top that dipped low at the front and tied at the side. Her feet were tucked into natural-colored pumps that added a couple inches to her height.

His gaze skimmed over her again, from top to bottom, and if he hadn't been so distracted by the mouthwatering sight of her shapely legs as she made her way toward him, he might have seen the steely glint in her eyes and anticipated her mood.

"Chez Henri?" she queried.

"Henry is my middle name," he explained.

"Any relation to Henry Garrett, of the furniture company?"

"My grandfather," he admitted.

"You're one of the Garrett Furniture Garretts," she said, somehow making the words an accusation rather than a statement.

He nodded. "Yes, I am."

"Which proves that I really am an idiot." She shook her head. "I knew your last name was Garrett, but it never occurred to me that you might have any connection to Garrett Furniture."

"Can we talk about this inside?" he suggested, because so long as she remained standing in his driveway, he knew she was thinking about getting back in her car and driving away.

She didn't respond to his question. Instead, she said, "We used the company as a case study in one of my business courses in college. Garrett Furniture was cited as an example of a small company that proved it was possible to grow and change and continue to be successful while still employing local people."

"My father will be pleased to hear that," he said. "But what I told you was the truth—I am a carpenter."

"For Garrett Furniture."

He shrugged. "It seemed disloyal to apply for a job somewhere else."

She didn't crack a smile. "I don't know you at all."

"You do," he insisted. "My connection to Garrett Furniture doesn't change anything. I just wanted a chance to get to know you without all the other stuff getting in the way."

"Other stuff?" she echoed, her tone filled with disbelief. "Would that other stuff be your job or your daughter? Or are there still other things that I don't know?"

"No, I think we've covered everything."

"Good." She nodded and turned back to the driveway.

He caught her arm and gently turned her around to face him again. "You came for lunch," he reminded her. "I'm not going to let you walk away hungry."

Rachel wasn't really hungry, and she knew that the longer she stayed the less likely she was to stick to her plan to say a final goodbye to him.

"I just put the rosemary chicken and potatoes into the oven."

"You cooked?"

He shook his head. "Sharlene prepped everything for me."

"Sharlene?"

"My housekeeper."

"You have a housekeeper," she said, and wondered why she was surprised. He was one of the Garrett Furniture Garretts—of course he had a housekeeper.

"I hired her after Nina died," he admitted. "I'm a lousy cook and I didn't want Maura to starve."

She let him lead her into the house, even though she knew it was probably a mistake. She shouldn't be here. She was happy with her life: she was a partner in a successful business—nothing even close to the scale of Garrett Furniture, but definitely holding its own—she lived in a nice if small apartment with a great view of Memorial Park, and she'd recently made the last payment on her car. Yes, she had a good life, but it didn't belong anywhere near his world.

A truth that became even clearer when she followed him down the wide hallway, peering into the doorways of the rooms they passed. Her first impression was that his house was surprisingly homey. It wasn't overdone or ostentatious, but the art on the walls and the heirloom carpets on the floor quietly whispered money, a sound that was echoed by the glossy antique tables and richly textured fabrics of the furniture.

And then she stepped into the kitchen.

Acres of glossy cherry-wood cabinets contrasted with miles of mushroom-colored quartz countertops, while the stainless steel handles on the cupboards and drawers coordinated with the top-of-the-line appliances, including a Sub-Zero refrigerator and dual-fuel range with double oven, six burners, charbroiler and griddle.

"You like to cook, don't you?" Andrew's voice was tinged with amusement.

She tore her gaze from the Rolls-Royce of ranges to look at him. "How can you tell?"

"You have that slightly glazed look in your eye that Jordyn gets whenever she comes in here."

Rachel smiled, but the truth was, she didn't just like to cook—she loved to cook and entertain. Unfortunately, neither was easy to do in her miniscule kitchen with basic amenities. In the limited space of her apartment, it was an accomplishment to put out cheese and crackers for half a dozen friends. If she was ever let loose in a kitchen like this, she was confident that she could put together a six-course meal for twice as many people.

"Whatever you paid for this house, I'd say it was worth it just for the kitchen," Rachel told him.

He chuckled and reached into the wine cooler—yes, there was actually a wine cooler built into the island—and pulled out a bottle of Riesling.

"I guess I did luck out. The previous owners, both serious chefs, had just completed the remodel when they found out the wife's company was transferring her to Singapore."

"That's quite the transfer."

He nodded. "They were motivated sellers."

"How long have you been here?"

"Almost two years." He showed her the label on the bottle. "Is this okay?"

She nodded, her thoughts on the timing of his move more than the wine. Somehow the realization that he hadn't shared this house with his wife helped her relax a little.

He deftly uncorked the bottle then poured the pale liquid into two elegant crystal glasses. She accepted the glass he offered, took a tiny sip, wary of the effect of any amount of alcohol on her already-precarious emotional state.

He checked the timer on the oven, then took her free hand and led her into the living room. Or maybe it was a parlor. She didn't think a house like his would have something as commonplace as a living room. Whatever it was called, it was warm and inviting.

There was a marble fireplace on one wall, flanked by tall windows covered in heavy brocade drapes. Flames crackled in the hearth, filling the room with warmth and light. It smelled pleasantly of leather and wood smoke with an underlying hint of lemon polish.

The longest wall boasted a couple of paintings, vibrantly colored landscapes in thick frames. Probably original works, undoubtedly valuable. But there were also photographs scattered around, mostly of Maura at various ages, some professionally posed shots but many more candid ones.

Rachel moved closer to the fire to look at the trio of

frames on the hearth. The first was a picture of Maura blowing bubbles through a wand. The second was Maura bundled up in a snowsuit beside a snowman that was nearly twice as big as she was. The third was of Andrew and Maura, sitting on a dock by the water, their feet dangling over the edge.

She took another sip of her wine and moved away from the fire.

"I know I screwed up," he said to her now. "But I'm asking for another chance."

"I can't be with someone who won't be honest with me," she told him.

He took her glass from her hand and set it on the table beside his. "Maybe I held back," he admitted. "Maybe I wanted to see if you were really interested in me for me and not my connection to the business."

She wanted to be offended that he would even think such a thing, but the truth was, he didn't know her well enough to know that his financial status wasn't a factor. So she could understand why he might have been reticent to disclose the truth about who he was. But—

"Why were you interested in me?"

She hadn't intended to speak the question out loud, but it had been churning in her mind since she'd pulled up in front of his house and realized exactly who he was, and it came spilling out now.

"You could have any woman you wanted—why do you want *me?*"

Chapter Eight

Andrew took a step closer, so that she was trapped between the couch at her back and his body in front. Then he leaned in, until his lips hovered just a few inches above hers. He lifted a hand, touched his fingertips to the pulse beneath her ear, then skimmed them down her throat, over her collarbone. Rachel's heart was pounding hard and fast, and he knew it.

"You're right," he finally said. "I probably could have any woman I wanted. That's not ego but fact, because most of the women I've gone out with don't really want me—they want access to the Garrett fortune and the lifestyle it can buy."

"And you thought I might be one of them?"

"Not once I got to know you," he assured her. "But the more I got to know you, the more I enjoyed being with you without my name getting in the way. It was…liberating.

"And the more I got to know you, the more I wanted you. I don't know if it was the sparkle in your eyes or the warmth in your smile that first got to me. I only know that I don't want any woman but you."

It was undeniably flattering, being the focus of his attention. It was also a little scary, because she knew that he meant it. Scarier still was the fact that she only wanted him.

"I started dating about six months ago—not because I was looking for a relationship but because I wanted to get my brothers off my back, to prove to them that I wasn't still grieving for Nina.

"I had a lot of first dates in those six months, but not one that I wanted to follow up with a second date. Until you.

"I was attracted to some of those other women, but I never wanted to take any one of them to my bed. Until you."

She swallowed. He was barely touching her, just the lightest caress of his fingertips over her skin. Just enough to make her want more.

She wanted him to kiss her; she wanted his hands on her, so that her mind would so completely cloud with lust that she wouldn't be able to think of all the reasons that this was a bad idea. But mostly she just wanted.

He brushed his lips against hers. It was the barest hint of a kiss, but still her knees trembled and her body yearned.

"But if you want me to back off, tell me that you don't want me as much as I want you."

She wanted to tell him exactly that, but he would know it was a lie. She did want him, every bit as much as he wanted her. What she didn't want was to have her heart broken again, but she knew that even if she ended it right now, she wasn't going to walk away unscathed.

"Wanting is the easy part," she said.

"Wanting you has been keeping me awake at night for weeks." He whispered the words against her mouth, then nibbled on the plump curve of her bottom lip. Her eyes closed, and a soft, needy sound whimpered in her throat.

He deepened the kiss, sliding his tongue between her lips. The distinctive male flavor went to her head more quickly than the wine. She lifted her hands to his chest, curled her fingers into his shirt for balance as the world tilted and spun. As he continued to kiss her, the wall she'd been trying to build between them crumbled.

He found the tie of her sweater at her waist, tugged the knot free. The fabric parted easily, and his hands dipped inside, stroking up her torso. His palms were rough, and the contrast against her bare skin made her shiver.

He eased his mouth from hers to trail kisses along her jaw, down her throat. His mouth was hot and wet on her flesh, his teeth scraped over her collarbone, his tongue traced the satin edging of her demi-cup bra. He tugged one of the straps down her arm, freeing her breast so that he could take her nipple in his mouth and suckle deeply. She felt moisture pool between her thighs, and the sharp ache of desire spread through her body. Her fingers sifted through his hair to cup the back of his head, holding him against her breast, wordlessly urging him to continue the exquisite pleasure.

His other hand moved under her skirt, over the silky nylons to the scalloped edge of her stay-up stockings. His fingers traced over the lacy detail, slowly, teasingly, until she shivered. "Andrew."

"Tell me what you want."

But she couldn't speak. She couldn't even think while he was touching her.

So he decided on his own course, and let his fingertips climb higher, skimming over the bare skin of her thighs, then to the wisp of fabric between them. He stroked a thumb over the satin and groaned when he found the material damp.

She was too aroused to feel embarrassed, and eager to touch him as he was touching her. Her hand slid down the front of his jeans, tracing the shape of his erection through the denim. He was rock-hard, and she trembled in response to this proof of his desire.

She tugged at the button of his pants, but he caught her hand in his and swore softly.

"What's wrong?"

"I don't have a condom," he admitted.

"Please tell me you're kidding."

He shook his head. "I didn't plan on this happening today. I didn't dare hope."

She leaned against the back of the couch and blew out an unsteady breath. She knew she should probably be grateful that he'd put the brakes on, but she couldn't help feeling disappointed.

"How far is the closest drugstore?"

His laughter was strained. "Too far."

"Damn," she muttered softly.

He brushed his lips against hers. "I promise that I won't be unprepared next time."

The idea of a next time was tempting, but she was still wary.

He took her hand, linked their fingers together. "Come on."

"Where are we going?"

"I promised you lunch," he reminded her, and then, almost on cue, the oven timer started to buzz.

Lunch was the roasted chicken and potatoes that he'd promised, along with a medley of vegetables and a salad of baby greens.

"I wish your housekeeper hadn't gone to so much trouble preparing lunch."

"Are you not enjoying it?"

"It's delicious," she assured him.

"But now you're feeling guilty about trying to dump me?" he guessed.

"You have to be in a relationship in order to be dumped," she pointed out.

"You don't think we have a relationship?"

"We went out exactly once."

"Twice."

"Valentine's Day wasn't a date."

"I asked you to go out and you said yes—to me, that's a date. Plus we had lunch at your shop, so we've actually had three dates."

"Okay, even if it was two or three dates—that doesn't make a relationship."

"What about what almost just happened in the living room?"

"A few dates and incredible chemistry still don't make a relationship."

"Why are you so resistant?" he asked. "You told me how close you are to your nephews, so it can't be that you don't like kids."

"I love kids," she admitted.

"But you don't like my daughter?"

"I don't know her," she pointed out.

"So spend some time with us, get to know her."

It was the obvious answer, but still she hesitated, unable to trust that he meant what he was saying, that he might actually be willing to let her all the way into his life—and into his daughter's life. She wanted to believe it, but she was wary. "It's not that simple."

"Why does it have to be complicated?"

"Because I don't do casual relationships," she admitted. "Even when I think I want to, I don't know how to hold back. And if I spend time with you—and with Maura— I'm afraid I'll fall in love with both of you."

His brows lifted. "You're afraid of falling in love?"

"I'm afraid of the splat that comes after the falling part."

"You think I'm going to hurt you?"

"No one ever goes into a relationship thinking that it's not going to work out."

"Then you're acknowledging that this is a relationship?"

She shook her head, equally charmed and frustrated by his persistence. "I'm acknowledging that it could turn into one."

"I haven't been in a relationship in a very long time," he reminded her. "I haven't wanted to be. But I want to give us a chance."

She'd have to be an idiot to say no. And not because he was Andrew Garrett of the Garrett Furniture Garretts but because of the way she felt when she was with him. He made her smile and laugh, and he listened when she talked, as if he really cared what she had to say and valued her opinion. Even when they were out in public, he was focused on her, as if she was the only person he wanted to be with. And if the way her body had responded to his touch in the living room was any indication, sex with Andrew would be off the charts.

But was she ready to take their relationship—if it was a relationship—to the next level? Was she ready to open up her heart? Because she'd never been good at sharing her body without giving her heart, and making herself that vulnerable again was a scary prospect.

"What do you say, Rachel?" he prompted.

Yes, opening her heart was scary, but she'd always said that if she was going to have regrets, she'd rather regret something she'd done than an opportunity she'd missed.

"Okay," she finally agreed.

He bent down to touch his lips to hers again. "And for that, you get dessert."

* * *

Andrew and Rachel had almost finished the apple caramel cheesecake Sharlene had made for dessert when he heard the front door open. As light footsteps raced down the hall, Rachel's gaze shifted to meet his. Before he could respond to her unspoken question, Maura skipped into the room.

"I'm home, Daddy," she announced.

The plan had been for Carol to pick her up from the birthday party when it ended at four o'clock, then he would get her from her grandparents after dinner. He didn't mind that she was home early, but he wasn't thrilled about the prospect of introducing his former mother-in-law to Rachel.

And although he wanted Rachel and Maura to spend some time together and get to know one another, he was a little wary. He didn't doubt that they would hit it off, but he was concerned about tempering his daughter's expectations. She'd been so excited after meeting Rachel the day before—it was practically the only thing she'd talked about from the time they left the movie theater until he tucked her into bed last night.

He'd wanted to make sure she understood that he and Rachel were going to be dating, but there were no guarantees it would lead to anything more. And if he could figure out some way to convince himself the same thing, even better. But the joy on Maura's face when she spotted Rachel warned that if he'd hoped to temper her expectations, he was already too late.

She gave him a hug and a kiss on the cheek, then climbed onto an empty chair and smiled shyly at Rachel. "Hi."

"How was your party?" Rachel asked her.

"It was good. We played games and had pizza and chips and cake."

"Sounds like fun."

Maura nodded. "But after the cake, I didn't feel so good."

"She wanted to come home because she had a tummy ache," Carol explained.

"Why didn't you call me?" Andrew asked his daughter.

"Jolene's mom said it was easier to take me to Grandma's."

"I didn't mind running her home," Carol assured him.

And he knew it was true. The Wakefields had always been willing and eager to help out with respect to their only grandchild, and he was usually grateful for their help.

He nodded, but kept his attention focused on his daughter. "Did the cake have strawberry filling?"

She shrugged.

"She has some food sensitivities that she isn't always careful about," he explained to Rachel. "Although thankfully nothing severe."

He turned back to his daughter. "Did it look like it might be strawberry?" he prompted.

"Maybe," she finally admitted.

He sighed. "Maura."

She pouted. "I didn't want to be the only one not having any. And I feel better now."

"Then you can come back to our house for dinner with me and Grandpa Ed, like we originally planned," Carol said.

But Maura shook her head. "I wanna stay here with Daddy and Rachel."

Andrew took that as his cue to introduce his former mother-in-law to his guest.

Rachel offered her hand to Maura's grandmother. Carol waited a beat before accepting, just long enough that the hesitation could not go unnoticed.

"You're a…friend…of Andrew's?" Carol asked, her tone cool.

"Yes, I am," Rachel confirmed.

"I wanna be friends, too," Maura said.

Her earnest statement tore at Andrew's heart, because it proved that no matter how hard he tried, he couldn't give his little girl everything she needed.

Rachel smiled at Maura. "I'd like that."

Carol, on the other hand, was looking anything but friendly. Andrew reminded himself that the older woman was Maura's grandmother, not his mother, and he didn't want or need her approval.

"I'll see you out," he said, and gestured for her to precede him to the foyer.

When he and Nina first started dating in high school, Carol had been less than supportive. Her mother had been a Du Pont, which meant that she didn't just come from money but old money, and she was unimpressed by Andrew's financial situation or social status. The fact that he worked with his hands had been another strike against him.

But Nina was their only child, and there wasn't anything she'd ever wanted that she didn't get. When she'd made it clear that she wanted Andrew, her parents had come around. And when Maura was born, he'd gone from being tolerated to respected as the father of their granddaughter. They'd been devastated when Nina died—and terrified that they would lose their granddaughter, too. But Andrew understood that Maura needed her grandparents and the connection to her mother that they represented as much as they needed her.

From the time she was two years old, Maura had spent one weekend a month with Carol and Ed. Nina and Andrew had appreciated the alone time that gave them, and they'd started talking about having another child just a few months before an aneurysm ruptured in her brain, taking her from her husband and daughter far too soon.

His former mother-in-law paused at the door and turned to face him. "I'm concerned, Andrew."

"About what?"

"Women parading in and out of your daughter's life."

The statement was so patently absurd that Andrew almost laughed out loud. "I don't know what you think constitutes a parade, Carol, but Rachel is the first woman I've ever invited into this house or introduced to my daughter."

His response didn't appease her. "Then why this one?" she asked him. "Why now?"

"I don't know," he admitted. "Maybe because I'm finally ready."

"I'm not a prude," Carol told him. "I understand that men have certain…needs."

He was tempted to challenge the implication that women didn't have the same needs, but that was definitely *not* a conversation he wanted to be having with Maura's grandmother, so he bit his tongue.

"If all I wanted from Rachel was sex, I wouldn't have brought her home to meet Maura."

"I just think it's too soon. I mean, how long have you even known this woman?"

"Too soon for whom?" he challenged, then shook his head, dismissing the question. "I appreciate that this is a difficult situation for you—"

"Do you?"

"I do," he assured her. "But my relationship with Rachel is none of your business."

Her lips thinned.

"Thank you again for bringing Maura home."

"There isn't anything I wouldn't do for my granddaughter," she assured him.

As Andrew closed the door behind her, it occurred to him that her statement sounded more threatening than reassuring.

While Andrew was occupied with his former mother-in-law, his daughter was busy spreading the goodies from her birthday party loot bag out on the table.

"There's some pretty cool stuff here," Maura said, nodding her head in approval.

Rachel surveyed the contents: purple bouncy ball, a bottle of bubble liquid, colorful ponytail holders, glittery nail stickers, a package of sugar-free bubble gum and a gift card for the movie theater.

"That is impressive," she agreed.

"Grandma says it's junk."

"Then I guess she won't want to share your bubble gum."

Maura giggled. "She doesn't chew bubble gum. 'It's unladylike,'" she said, in a fair imitation of Carol Wakefield's superior tone.

There was plenty that Rachel could say in response to that, but she bit her tongue. Whatever her impression of the older woman, she was the little girl's grandmother.

"What's going on in here?" Andrew demanded, standing in the doorway with his fists on his hips. "Do I hear giggles? You know the rules—there are no giggles allowed, young lady."

Of course, his mock severity only made the child giggle some more.

"Look what I got, Daddy," she said, gesturing to the scattering of items.

"Wow. It almost looks like it was *your* birthday."

"Next time we go to the movies, I can buy my own ticket," she told him.

"And mine?"

"Maybe Rachel's, too," she said.

Andrew ruffled her hair. "You're feeling better now?"

She nodded. "Can we play a game?"

He looked at Rachel. "What do you think?"

"Please," Maura added.

Rachel knew she should go home and let Andrew have some quiet time with his daughter, but the little girl was looking at her so beseechingly, there was no way she could refuse. "What kind of game?"

"We have Candy Land," Andrew said.

Maura wrinkled her nose. "Candy Land's for babies."

"What do you want to play?" her father asked her.

"Five Card Draw."

Rachel's brows lifted. "You want to play poker?"

"My brother babysat one night and turned her into a card shark," Andrew explained.

Maura grinned proudly.

"I'm not sure I know how to play poker," Rachel admitted.

"I'll teach you," the little girl said.

Andrew retrieved a deck of cards and a tray of poker chips from the dining room sideboard. While he shuffled the cards, Maura explained the basics to Rachel.

"The dealer gives you five cards. You look at your cards and decide what you wanna keep or trade—but you can't trade any more than three.

"Unless you've gotta ace," she clarified. "Then you can show your ace and trade the rest.

"After everyone has made their bets—that's putting a chip in the middle of the table—the new cards are dealt and the best hand gets all the chips."

"How do I know what's the best hand?" Rachel asked.

"I need help with that, too," Maura admitted, then went to a drawer in the sideboard and pulled out a wrinkled piece of paper. "I can never remember if a straight beats a flush, so Uncle Nate made me a chart."

So Rachel spent the next hour playing poker with Andrew and his daughter—and the little girl trounced the adults soundly every time. Even when Rachel was feeling pretty confident looking at the four sixes in her hand, Maura bested her by laying down four tens.

"She has to be cheating," Andrew lamented, tossing his cards onto the table. "No one is that lucky all the time."

"I don't cheat," Maura said indignantly. "Uncle Nate says it's just the luck of the draw."

Andrew pushed his chair away from the table as the phone started ringing. "He probably cheats, too."

While he went to the other room to take the call, Rachel gathered up the cards. "Maybe we should play Candy Land next time," she said. "I'm pretty good at that game."

"You really like Candy Land?" the little girl asked.

"It was one of my favorite games when I was a kid."

"I didn't know it was that old," Maura said, so solemnly that Rachel couldn't help but laugh.

"Even my mother played Candy Land when she was a little girl," she told the child.

"Do you still have a mommy?"

She nodded, suddenly aware that her innocent comment might have opened a whole can of worms.

"My mommy's dead," Maura told her.

Rachel nodded again. "I know. I'm sorry."

"But maybe, someday, I could get a new mommy."

No, not just one can of worms—a crate filled with cans, Rachel decided. "Maybe you will," she said lightly.

"But she'll have to be someone my daddy likes."

"That would probably help," she agreed.

"Daddy likes you," Maura said.

Thankfully Andrew's return prevented her from taking the conversation any further.

Chapter Nine

Maura had a secret.

A big secret. So big it felt like it filled up everything inside of her until she might burst if she didn't tell somebody.

She decided to tell Kristy, because she was her best friend and best friends told each other everything. When the bell rang to indicate the start of recess, they grabbed their coats and headed out to the playground. They were only halfway across the field when the secret burst out of her.

"My dad has a girlfriend."

Kristy stopped dead, her eyes big. "Really?"

Maura nodded. "Her name's Rachel, and she has brown hair and blue eyes and she smells like vanilla cupcakes."

"Are they gonna get married?"

The question dimmed her excitement, just a little. "I don't know."

Kristy continued toward the monkey bars, and Maura fell into step beside her. "My mom's getting married to her boyfriend and I get to be a flower girl in the wedding and then I'm gonna get a baby brother or sister."

Maura already knew all of that because Kristy told her the same thing almost every day. Except the baby part. She thought that might be new.

"Maybe my daddy and Rachel will have a baby, and then I can be a flower girl, too."

"They hafta get married before they have the baby," Kristy said as she swung herself up onto the top of the structure.

Maura sat down on top of the steps her friend had just climbed. "How come?"

Kristy hooked her feet through the bars and let herself fall back, so she was hanging upside down, her arms dangling toward the ground. Maura could do the same thing, but Mrs. Patterson said it was dangerous. If the teacher caught her, she'd get in trouble. Kristy didn't care about getting in trouble.

"'Cuz that's how it works," her friend explained.

Maura wished she knew half the stuff that Kristy did.

"Oh—and they hafta kiss," Kristy said, as if she'd just remembered that part.

"'Cuz kissing means they really like each other."

Kristy looked funny nodding while she was upside down.

"I think my daddy kissed Rachel."

"Didya see it?"

She shook her head.

"You hafta see it to know for sure." The bell rang to signal the end of recess, and Kristy dropped down from the bars.

Maura decided that she would watch more closely the next time Rachel came over.

When Andrew and Rachel started dating, it had occurred to him that Maura might be resistant to him spending time with another woman. For more than three years, it had been just the two of them. She spent time with each set of grandparents, of course, and with his brothers and various cousins, but no one else—aside from Sharlene—had been part of their day-to-day ritual. As a result, he wouldn't have been surprised if she'd balked at any change in that routine.

It didn't take long for him to realize that his concerns were completely unfounded. Not only did Maura not mind when he included Rachel in their plans, she was disappointed if a day went by that she didn't see her. His daughter's easy acceptance of and obvious affection for Rachel should have eased his mind... So why did it make him *un*easy?

He was torn—not about his feelings for Rachel. Those were unequivocal. He wanted her with an intensity that he couldn't ever remember experiencing before. Of course, the more than three years that he'd gone without sex might have something to do with it, but he suspected that Rachel herself was the biggest factor.

"So tell me about her."

He looked up to find his mother in the doorway of his office. "Who?"

"Whoever is responsible for that smile on your face."

He scrambled for a plausible explanation. "Our sales rep in Alabama."

She shook her head. "No way were you thinking about business."

"I never could fool you, could I?"

She went to the coffeepot on the other side of the room and poured herself a cup, a sure sign that she was settling in for a chat.

He held back a sigh. "Her name is Rachel Ellis."

She brought the pot to his desk and topped up his cup,

then lowered herself into a chair across from him. And because she was his mother, he found himself opening up.

"She's… I know this sounds corny, but she's unlike any other woman I've ever known. She's beautiful and sexy, but it's more than that. There's just something about her that when I'm with her…she makes everything brighter."

Jane smiled. "She makes you happy."

"Yes, she does."

"How long have you been seeing her?"

"A couple of weeks."

"Has Maura met her?"

He nodded. "Yes."

"How did that go?"

"Well, once Rachel got over the shock that I had a child, it went well. She's great with Maura—comfortable and natural. And Maura absolutely adores her."

"And that worries you," she guessed.

"A little." He picked up his mug, sipped his coffee. "Maybe more than a little."

"Why?"

"Because I didn't realize how much Maura missed having a mother. Because I tried so hard to do everything right—to be everything she needed."

"You're a wonderful father."

The conviction in her tone made him smile, until he remembered, "But Maura wants a mother."

"Oh." She sipped her coffee. "She told you this?"

He nodded.

"Before or after she met Rachel?"

"Before. When she learned that her best friend's mom getting married again meant that Kristy was getting a new dad."

"That's not so surprising," Jane assured him. "She's an almost-seven-year-old girl who wants a 'real' family like her friends."

"I know," he agreed. "But now…I can see the hope shining in her eyes every time she looks at Rachel. And I know she isn't thinking about a mother in abstract terms anymore—she wants Rachel to be that mother."

"Is Rachel not interested?"

"I don't know. We've only been dating a few weeks—it seems a little premature to even be asking those questions."

"Maybe for most people," she acknowledged. "But your situation is different."

"Because I have a child to think about."

She shook her head. "No. I mean, yes, of course, you do. But that isn't what I meant."

"What did you mean?"

"Of all my children, you're most like me—you lead with your heart, even if you don't realize it."

He scowled at that.

She laughed. "A son never wants to hear that he's like his mother, does he? But it's not a bad thing, Andrew. You fell in love with Nina so quickly—and even though we cautioned that you were both too young, your feelings didn't change. Even when you went away to different schools, you remained steadfast and loyal. You were seventeen when you decided that you were going to marry her and, ten years later, you did.

"I didn't think you would ever get over losing her," Jane said softly. "And it broke my heart to see how badly you were hurting and know there was nothing I could do to help. Thankfully you had Maura, and you were able to pull it together for her, because you knew that she needed you.

"But you lived in limbo for a long time. I know it was partly because you were grieving and partly because you were so focused on your duties as a father you couldn't think about anything else. I'm happy to see that you've opened your heart and are actually living again."

He wasn't sure he agreed with her summary of the situation. His history with Nina was indisputable, but she was getting way ahead of herself with respect to his feelings for Rachel. Right now, he was just trying to take things one day at a time.

"So when do I get to meet her?" Jane asked.

"I'll keep you posted."

Of course, she wasn't satisfied with that vague response. "Sunday," she decided.

"Any Sunday in particular?"

"This Sunday. Bring her to dinner."

"I'm not sure she's ready to meet the family," he hedged.

"Or that you're ready for her to meet the family?"

"Maybe."

"Look at it this way," his mother suggested. "If she hangs around until dessert, you'll know she has staying power."

The more time Rachel spent with Andrew and Maura, the more she began to realize that her concerns had been unfounded. Whenever he and his daughter planned an outing, they invited her to go, too. Aside from Maura's gymnastics classes and piano lessons, they didn't venture out very often during the week. Andrew was diligent about the child's eight o'clock bedtime on school nights, and that was okay with Rachel. It didn't matter to her what they did; she just enjoyed being with them.

But one Wednesday night, in celebration of the perfect grade Maura had received on her spelling test, Andrew decided they should go out for dinner. He let his daughter choose the venue and she decided on Valentino's.

Rachel had been wary about joining them, worried that Gemma might make too much of the fact that they were together. As it turned out, Gemma had taken the night off, so Marco was filling in for her.

Rachel was relieved to avoid a steely-eyed interrogation

from her friend and pleased, as always, to see Gemma's charming brother-in-law.

He lifted her hand and touched his lips to the back of it. "You get more beautiful every time I see you," he told her.

"And your flirtation skills are more polished every time I see you."

"Are you alone tonight?" He flashed the smile that had no doubt made countless female hearts sigh. "Because I would be happy to neglect my duties and share a glass of vino with you."

"Then we would both face Gemma's wrath," she warned him. "And actually, I'm meeting…friends."

She glanced around the dining room, looking to see if Andrew and Maura were already there. She spotted him almost immediately.

Marco sighed. "Ah, *bella,* you're breaking my heart."

"The extensive trail of ex-girlfriends behind you would suggest your heart is indestructible."

"I used to think so," he agreed. "Until I saw the way you smiled at him. Obviously he makes you happy."

"He does," she agreed.

"You let me know if that ever changes."

She laughed. "Not in this lifetime, Marco."

He guided her to the table where Andrew and Maura were seated.

Rachel and Andrew both ordered the penne with sausage and peppers; Maura had the three-cheese ravioli. While they ate, Maura happily regaled the adults with stories about recent happenings at school, most of them centering on her best friend, Kristy, with the occasional reference to other classmates and their teacher, Mrs. Patterson.

"Anyone for dessert?" Marco asked, when he'd cleared away their plates.

"Ice cream," Maura immediately replied. Then she turned to her father. "Please, Daddy. Can I have ice cream?"

"I think a perfect spelling test warrants a reward," Andrew agreed.

"With chocolate sauce and the cookie bits and whipped cream," Maura told the waiter. "No strawberries."

"Did I hear correctly—did you write a perfect spelling test?" Marco asked the little girl.

She nodded.

"No mistakes at all?"

She shook her head.

"In that case, you are entitled to exclusive, behind-the-scenes access to frozen dairy delights."

Maura's eyes went wide. "What does that mean?"

He bent down to whisper closer to her ear. "It means that you get to come into the kitchen to make your own sundae."

"Really?"

"Absolutely," Marco confirmed. "As long as your dad says it's okay."

"Can I, Daddy?"

"Sure," he agreed.

Marco pulled back her chair for her and offered his hand. Rachel had to smile, amused by this proof that he could charm females of any age. Or maybe it was Maura who had charmed Marco, she considered, as they went off together to the kitchen.

"You have a truly wonderful daughter," she said to Andrew.

"I've been warned that will probably change when she hits puberty."

"It probably will," Rachel agreed. "But for now, simple things like ice-cream sundaes and sleepovers still put a smile on her face."

"I don't know what I was thinking when I agreed to the latter," he admitted.

"You were thinking that it would make her happy."

"I was," he agreed. "But I'd be a lot happier if I was the one having a friend sleep over."

Her brows lifted. "Any friend in particular?"

His hand settled on her thigh, beneath the tablecloth. "One name in particular comes to mind."

"Maybe Kristy's mom will reciprocate and invite Maura to stay at her house next week."

Before he could respond to that, Maura came back with her ice cream in an old-fashioned tulip glass: two scoops of vanilla dripping with gooey chocolate sauce, sprinkled with cookie crumbles, toffee bits and mini-M&M's with a mountain of whipped cream topped with three cherries.

"Three cherries?" Andrew said.

Maura grinned. "One for me, one for you and one for Rachel."

Friday night, the night of Maura's sleepover, Rachel decided to make her own plans. But Holly had a date, most of her other friends were working or already had other plans, and even her nephews were busy, leaving her to her own devices. She didn't really mind. She'd been working long hours lately and spending almost every free minute she had with Andrew and Maura, so she figured it was a good idea to give herself some space.

After she closed up the shop, she went to Buy The Book to pick up her favorite author's latest release. When she got home, she was surprised to find Andrew's car parked in one of the visitor spots by her apartment building. And the man himself standing outside the doors.

"I was in the neighborhood and thought I'd stop by to see what you were doing tonight."

"My plans include leftover lasagna, a glass of Chianti

and—" she held up the book she carried "—a date with Eve and Roarke."

"Could I tempt you to change those plans with the offer of a juicy steak, a glass of merlot and a date with me?"

More than the meal, she was tempted by the idea of being with him. "I thought Maura's sleepover was tonight."

"It was," he agreed. "Until Kristy woke up with chicken pox this morning."

"Oh." It was all too easy to imagine how Maura had responded to that news. "She must be so disappointed."

"She was. And then my mom called, and when she heard about the change in Maura's plans, she invited her to spend the night at Grandma and Grandpa's house. In fact, I just dropped her off there and took a chance that I might catch you here."

"And you did."

"And are you going to let me talk you into coming back to my place for that steak dinner?"

"Your place...where no one else is home?"

"No one," he confirmed.

She knew what he was asking, and that dinner was only the first part of it.

"What do you think?"

"I think there's no one home at my place, either," she told him. "And it's a lot closer than yours."

As she punched the button for the seventh floor, Rachel felt her stomach twist into knots. She'd been thinking about this moment for weeks, wanting this moment, wanting him. But now that it was imminent, she was inexplicably nervous.

Then, as the elevator began its ascent, Andrew reached for her hand and linked their fingers together. And somehow that simple contact settled her.

Because this was Andrew—a man she knew and

trusted. A man who read to his daughter every night before bed and had dinner with his own parents every other Sunday. A man who called her half an hour after kissing her goodbye just because he wanted to hear her voice. A man who turned her inside out with his kisses, who knew she wanted him as much as he wanted her and still understood that this was a huge deal for her.

She unlocked the door and stepped inside, setting her book down on the coffee table and her keys on top of it.

Should she lead him down the hall straight to her bedroom? Or should she offer him a drink first? Or maybe—

He tipped her chin up and brushed his lips lightly over hers. "Second thoughts?"

She shook her head because she had no doubts about what she wanted, even if her stomach was tangled up with knots and nerves.

"This is a big step for me, too," he told her.

"Really?"

He nodded. "I haven't been with anyone since..." He trailed off, offered her a shrug and a crooked smile. "Since."

She realized the he didn't want to speak his wife's name and risk her coming between them. She appreciated his consideration, and she was just a little intimidated by the implication.

If he hadn't been with anyone since Nina had died, more than three years earlier, that certainly trumped her now seventeen months of celibacy. And the fact that he was willing to take this step with her proved that she meant something to him.

"Now I'm even more nervous," she admitted.

"We can take it as slow as you want," he promised.

"What I want right now is for you to kiss me."

He immediately complied with her request.

The kiss started out gentle, reassuring, and the knots

in her belly began to loosen. When she was in his arms, it was as if the rest of the world faded away so that there was only the two of them, and she only wanted him to go on kissing her forever. She was certain if he did, she wouldn't ever want or need anything else.

But eventually the tenor of the kiss changed, desire turned to need. Hot, achy and desperate. His arms tightened around her, so that she was pressed against him, from shoulder to thigh and all the erogenous zones in between. Suddenly she wasn't feeling nervous anymore—just needy.

She tore her mouth from his. "I think we should save *slow* for later," she said, taking his hand to lead him to her bedroom.

She turned on the lamp beside the bed, so that soft light pushed away the darkness. He should have looked out of place in her distinctly feminine room with its empire rosette sleigh bed piled with decorative pillows and the elegant lines of the Queen Anne dressers and lacy window coverings. Instead, the feminine trappings only seemed to enhance his masculinity.

She had a moment to wish that she'd thought to set candles around the room, just in case. But she hadn't planned for this to happen. Certainly not this soon. Maybe she should turn on some music...or get the wine...

Slowly he turned her around, so that she was in his arms again. And the way he was looking at her, she realized none of that mattered. All that mattered was what was between them, the attraction that had drawn them inexorably closer over the past several weeks, leading toward this moment.

She started to unfasten the top button of her shirt, but he covered her hands with his own. "I want to do that."

His voice was husky and filled with promise.

"Okay." She let her hands drop back to her side.

His eyes, dark and intense, held hers as he worked the

buttons free. His fingers fumbled a little and, surprisingly, that evidence of his nerves helped settle her own. As the front of her shirt opened, the backs of his knuckles brushed against her skin, making her shiver, making her yearn.

At first she welcomed the cool rush of air on her heated flesh, until she realized that her skin being exposed meant that he could see her exposed skin.

She immediately pushed his hands away and tried to cover herself again. "Wait."

Chapter Ten

Wait?

Andrew blew out an unsteady breath and curled his fingers in his palms to stop himself from reaching for her again. "Why are we waiting?"

It was hard to tell in the dim light, but Rachel's cheeks seemed to flush. "I need to change."

He lifted a brow. "Change…your clothes?"

She nodded.

"Why?" he asked, sincerely baffled.

"Because I bought new lingerie," she finally admitted.

"So you're not putting on the brakes? You haven't changed your mind about this…you just want to put on different underwear?"

The color in her cheeks deepened. "It sounds ridiculous when you say it like that, but yes."

It was ridiculous, but he didn't figure saying so would result in her getting naked any quicker. It was also flattering, that she'd bought something special in anticipation of this event. But after his extended period of celibacy, the prospect of seeing her naked was far more arousing than anything she might put on her body. "Don't you realize that it doesn't matter what you're wearing because my end goal is to take it off you?"

"But I want to look sexy when you're taking it off me."

He stroked her hair away from her face. "You are sexy. So incredibly and undeniably sexy. And while I'm flattered that you bought new lingerie in anticipation of showing it to me, I'm much more interested in your naked body than anything made of satin or lace that would only cover it up."

"Maybe it was leather with buckles and chains."

His brows lifted. "Was it?"

"No," she admitted.

"Okay, then," he said, and pried her fingers from the blouse that she was clutching in front of her like a shield.

He slid the garment down her arms and let it fall to the floor. The bra she wore was white, but it wasn't boring. He knew enough about women's lingerie to recognize it as a demi-cup bra, and he appreciated the contrast of the snowy satin against her creamy flesh. Even more, he appreciated that the center clasp hidden beneath a tiny bow was easily released.

He dropped the bra on top of her already-discarded blouse and focused his attention on the mouthwatering sight of her naked breasts. More than three years without physical intimacy seemed to have given him a whole new appreciation for the uniqueness of the female body. Or maybe it was the uniqueness of Rachel's body that so completely captivated him.

He'd been married for five years, but even prior to that, he'd never been with anyone but Nina. So while he might have plenty of experience with sex, that experience had all been with the same woman. Being with someone different—with Rachel—was like the first time all over again.

His heart was pounding and everything inside of him was shaking with excitement and anticipation and terror. He wanted her so desperately that he couldn't help worrying he would forget patience and finesse, that he might do something wrong and screw everything up.

His gaze skimmed over her, assessing, admiring. "Incredibly and undeniably sexy," he said again.

The way he looked at her—the unrestrained desire she could see in his eyes—made Rachel feel sexy. And when he lifted his hands to her breasts, cupping their weight in his palms, as if they were unique and precious, she knew he saw her that way.

But he didn't linger there. His hands skimmed down her sides to the waistband of her pants. It took him a minute to find the fastener and unhook it, then he lowered the zipper and pushed her pants over her hips, adding them to the growing pile of discarded clothing on the floor. Her panties and stockings soon followed.

Then he stepped back to look at her, and his voice was filled with reverence when he said, "Yes—that's how I want you."

"I want you naked, too," she told him.

"Soon," he promised. "First I want to touch every inch of you…with my hands…and my lips."

His fingers skimmed over her skin as he spoke, leaving goose bumps along her flesh. She was hot and cold, and desperate for him.

Then he dipped his head to brush his lips along her collarbone, and she shivered.

He lifted his head. "Cold?"

She shook her head as he eased her back onto the bed. "You are so beautiful."

Right now, she was so turned on.

Her nipples were already peaked, begging for his attention, and he didn't disappoint. He swirled his tongue around one turgid point, and she gasped in response to the wet heat of his mouth on her bare skin. Then he shifted to the other breast, drew the nipple into his mouth and suckled deeply.

She reached for him, tugging his shirt out of his pants, desperate to put her hands on him.

He kissed her again, slowly and deeply, as his hands skimmed over her, tracing every dip and curve of her body. Then his mouth followed the same path, his lips and tongue stroking and teasing.

"Andrew...please."

"That's what I'm trying to do," he told her.

What he was doing was driving her insane.

"I thought we were saving *slow* for later," she said.

"That was your idea, not mine." He swirled his tongue around her navel, making the muscles in her belly quiver. "I've wanted you for too long to rush this."

He nipped at her hip, kissed the inside of her thigh. "Although I should probably warn you, the actual act is probably going to be over sooner than I would like."

She was on the edge, teetering on the brink. "Could you please stop apologizing in advance and just get on with it?"

"I want to make sure you're ready." And he parted the soft folds at her center, groaning in appreciation when he discovered that she was already wet.

"I'm more than ready."

He licked the sensitive flesh, and she whimpered. He nibbled some more, tasting, teasing. He didn't seem to be in any hurry, but Rachel was quickly growing impatient. She wanted him inside of her, moving with her toward the ultimate pinnacle of pleasure. She wanted...

Oh. Wow. Yes.

Fireworks of sensation shot through her body as his tongue delved into her, then flicked over the tight bud at her center, alternating quick licks with slow strokes, pushing her relentlessly toward the edge…closer…closer…and…over.

"I think you're ready," he finally decided, and she managed to choke out a laugh.

He quickly stripped away his clothes, almost tripping over his pants in his haste to get rid of them. She muffled her giggle. But when he faced her in his full naked glory, she didn't feel like laughing at all. He fumbled a little in tearing open the condom packet, and his hands weren't entirely steady as he sheathed himself, reminding her of what he'd said about it being a long time for him, too.

When he was finally ready, he levered himself over her on the bed and spread her legs wide. She lifted her hips off the mattress, desperate to have him inside of her. His arms were braced on the mattress, holding himself in position over her as tiny beads of perspiration formed on his brow, proof of his intense focus. She reached between their bodies and wrapped her fingers around the hard length of him, and his eyes closed on a heartfelt groan of appreciation as she guided him home.

Her own sound of pleasure echoed his as he eased into her, deep, deeper, and the sensation of his hard length buried inside of her was enough to start the fireworks again. She cried out, her nails digging into his shoulders as the orgasm ripped through her. He held himself perfectly still, his arms rigid and his jaw tight, and she knew he was fighting to control his own response as her muscles pulsed and contracted around him.

She wanted him to let go, to give himself up to the pleasure of their joining as she had. But he held on, and when the aftershocks finally faded, he began to move inside of her. Slow, deep strokes that seemed to touch her very core. And though she wouldn't have thought it was possible, the pressure started to build yet again.

She dug her heels into the mattress, lifting her hips to meet him, thrust for thrust. Harder. Faster. Deeper.

She arched. Clenched. Released.

This time, when she flew, he went with her.

Three years was a long time to go without sex.

For the first year, Andrew hadn't thought too much about it—the pain of losing his wife had made him oblivious to all else. Eventually, though, as his heart began to heal, those basic needs had stirred again. But none of the women he knew had piqued his interest enough to want to do anything about satisfying those needs.

Now, he was very definitely satisfied.

When he finally summoned the energy to lift himself off Rachel, he whacked his heel on the footboard. He'd never considered himself particularly graceful, but he'd never thought he was as clumsy as he'd been since walking into Rachel's bedroom. He swore, mostly under his breath, as the pain radiated through his foot, and she chuckled softly.

"I bet you have a king-size bed, don't you?"

"I do," he admitted.

"Maybe we should have gone to your place."

"Right now, I don't want to be anywhere else but right where I am," he said, wrapping his arm around her and snuggling her close to his body.

She smiled. "That sounds like a man who just got lucky."

"Very, very lucky," he told her, and meant it.

He'd missed the fragrant softness of a woman's body. He'd missed the joy and challenge of exploring all of her dips and curves to discover what made her sigh, what made her gasp, what made her scream. He smiled, pleased that he'd already found a few of Rachel's secret spots—and was looking forward to finding many more.

But first, he needed fuel. "Do you have enough of that leftover lasagna to share?"

"If I throw together a salad and add garlic bread."

He opened the wine while she made the salad, and after they ate, they made love again.

He ducked into the bathroom to dispose of the condom. Two minutes later, he returned to her bedroom and just a glimpse of her naked body tangled in the sheets had his body stirring again.

He climbed back into the bed and kissed her softly.

She smiled at him. "Are you going to stay?"

"Were you planning on kicking me out?"

"No, but I do have the early shift tomorrow," she warned.

"There's still a lot of hours between now and tomorrow," he said, stroking his hands over her sleek curves.

"I was hoping to spend at least some of those hours sleeping."

"Later," he promised, as he parted her thighs and slipped into the welcoming haven between them.

She fell asleep in his arms and woke up the same way.

His left arm was wrapped around her waist, and when she glanced down she could see the faint line around his third finger.

She didn't begrudge the fact that he'd been married, or even that he'd obviously loved his wife. But that circle of pale skin made her wonder if she would ever come first for any man. Even if Andrew did love her, would he love her as much as he'd loved Nina? Would he—

Her breath caught in her throat when his hand shifted a little higher. His fingers toyed with her nipple, and he snuggled closer, making her aware of the fact that he was very definitely awake.

"Next to sex, I think this is what I missed most of all—waking up with a sexy woman in my arms," he told her.

"I have bedhead and morning breath."

"You're perfect," he said, and captured her mouth in a slow and very thorough kiss that proved he meant it.

"I have to go into work," she reminded him.

"What time?"

"Seven." She wriggled out of his embrace and reached for her robe.

He glanced at the clock. "Then we still have almost an hour."

"I have to shower."

"I can multitask," he promised, scooping her into his arms and carrying her into the bathroom.

Rachel was feeling relaxed and happy when she unlocked the shop at 7:10 a.m. She was running a little bit behind schedule, which was completely out of character for her, and she didn't even care. Not even the surly attitude of the deliveryman, who'd apparently been waiting those ten minutes, fazed her.

When Holly came in at ten o'clock, she took one look at her friend and said, "Are you on happy pills?"

"Nope."

"Then you got lucky last night."

"Very, very lucky," she said, borrowing Andrew's response, then grinned. "And again this morning."

"I guess I don't need to ask how it was."

"It was...so much more than I expected."

"Either your expectations were too low or he was really good."

"Do you remember when you asked me if I could top five?"

Holly's gaze narrowed suspiciously. "No way."

Rachel nodded. "Seven," she said proudly.

"Wow."

"That's what I said…when I finally regained the power of speech."

"No wonder you're grinning like a crazy person."

"I feel good today," Rachel admitted. "Happy."

"I'm glad. Just…be careful."

"Thanks, but I remember the safe-sex spiel from high school."

"I'm not talking about protecting your body but your heart."

"It was one night," she reminded her friend.

"And you're more than halfway in love with him already."

"I am not."

She enjoyed being with Andrew, but she wasn't going to make the mistake of planning a future for them together when they'd only been dating a few weeks.

At least she hoped she wasn't.

After work on Saturday, Rachel drove to Raleigh to pick up her nephews. Since this sleepover had been planned for several weeks, she didn't expect to see Andrew or Maura that night. But just as the boys were debating pizza or pasta for dinner, Maura called.

She explained that they were having a movie marathon at her house—with both of the *Cars* movies—and since they weren't girl movies, maybe Rachel and "her boys" could come over to watch. Trent immediately said yes, but Scott, who tended to be the shyer of the two, hesitated. He was more interested in pizza than a movie, so when Maura said that they were having pizza, too, he was persuaded.

"What are your plans for tomorrow?" Andrew asked, when the pizza was gone and the kids were settled down in front of the giant-screen TV in his media room.

"I promised to take Scott and Trent to the Marbles Kids Museum."

"Do you mind if Maura and I tag along?"

"Of course not. But I have to have the boys home by four, because they're going to Kim's parents for dinner."

"That's convenient," he said, latching onto the opening she'd given him. "Because you've been invited to come for Sunday dinner at my parents' house."

She swallowed. "You're inviting me to meet your family?"

"They're mostly harmless," he assured her.

"But we've only been dating a few weeks."

"I want you to meet my family—and I know they want to meet you."

"What did you tell them about me?" she asked warily.

"I didn't tell them anything until my mother cornered me at work this week and demanded to know why I was so happy, which led to your name coming up and her insisting that I invite you to Sunday dinner."

She'd been with Eric for a year and a half but had never met his parents. In fact, she'd only met his daughter after they'd been dating for six months—and she'd been introduced to his ex-wife at the same time because Wendy had insisted on being present when Summer met Rachel.

She probably should have realized then that her relationship with Eric was doomed. Or at least when she commented to him about the little touches and the secret smiles his ex was always giving him and he'd accused her of overreacting. Wendy might have chosen to end their marriage, but she still wanted to control her ex-husband. And he let her.

The more time she spent with Andrew and Maura, the more she realized how mistaken she'd been to ever compare him with her ex. He wanted her to have a good relationship with his daughter and happily included Rachel in their family activities. No, there were no problems from that sector—the problems were with the little girl's maternal grandmother.

And now Andrew wanted her to meet the paternal grandparents. While she didn't expect they would have the same issues as Carol Wakefield—who was undoubtedly trying to hold on to her only remaining link with her own child—she suspected that she would still be under the microscope, examined and compared, even if subconsciously, to the woman Andrew had married. And it was her own doubts and insecurities that made her worry they would find her lacking.

"Yes? No?" Andrew prompted.

"Is 'no' an option?"

"Not really. My mother's sent me six text messages in the past twenty-four hours pressing for confirmation that you'll be there."

"Then I guess I'll be there," she agreed.

But she managed to put it out of her mind—mostly—while they were at the museum with the kids.

She was surprised to learn that Maura had never been there before. Of course, because her nephews lived in Raleigh, it was one of their favorite places, and they were thrilled to show Maura around.

They dressed up in costumes and played with building blocks and explored an obstacle course and pushed around life-size chess pieces. Most importantly, they had fun. And when it was time to take the boys home, none of them wanted to leave.

After she'd dropped off Scott and Trent, they stopped at Buds & Blooms on the way to his parents' house so that Rachel could put together a pretty arrangement for his mother. Maura was fascinated by the numerous buckets of flowers, so she let the little girl pick out the ones she wanted to give to Grandma Jane. After she'd selected the appropriate greenery to add to the bouquet, she showed Maura how to tie the stems together with twine then wrapped it in clear cellophane.

David and Jane Garrett's house wasn't in the exclusive Forrest Hill neighborhood, as she'd expected. Instead, their ten acres of property straddled the border between Parkhurst and Westdale, on the southwest side of town. It was an old and established area, and the houses there had been built before developers started to cram enormous structures onto postage-stamp-size lots. Andrew explained that the house was actually an old farmhouse, renovated and added on to so many times over the years that it bore little resemblance to the original structure.

"My father keeps offering to buy—or build—something new, but my mother refuses. Because they bought the house when they were newlyweds and each of us kids took our first steps in that house."

His father was a big man—easily as tall as Andrew and just as broad across the shoulders. He had dark hair liberally sprinkled with gray at the temples, the same green eyes as his eldest son, a quick smile and a firm handshake.

His mother was tiny in comparison to her husband. Maybe five-four, Rachel guessed, with a slight build, chin-length blond hair and blue eyes. She didn't offer her hand. Instead, she enfolded Rachel in her embrace.

"I'm so pleased to finally meet you."

"Thank you for inviting me to dinner," Rachel said, offering her the flowers.

"Oh, my, these are beautiful."

"I helped make the bouquet," Maura said proudly.

"Then you should help me find a vase to put them in," her grandmother suggested.

Maura took her hand and skipped off to the kitchen.

"Are Nathan and Daniel here?" Andrew asked his father.

"In the family room watching some game on TV. Kenna's there, too."

"Kenna's a friend of Daniel's from high school," Andrew explained, leading Rachel to the family room to introduce her to his brothers.

She wasn't surprised that Andrew's brothers were good-looking. She was surprised how similar they were to one another, in height, build and appearance. She knew Andrew was the eldest, but he wasn't the tallest. His youngest brother, Daniel, had about half an inch on him, and maybe a full inch on middle brother, Nathan.

Nathan's hair was a little darker than both of his brothers, his eyes were gray rather than green, and dimples flashed when he smiled. Daniel had a slightly peaked hairline, stubble on his square jaw and a devil-may-care sparkle in his emerald eyes. Kenna was quite possibly the most beautiful woman Rachel had ever met. With pale blond hair, big blue eyes, a dazzling smile and long, lean curves. She looked like a Swedish swimsuit model—generally the type of woman any other female wanted to hate on principle, except that she was also genuinely warm and friendly.

When Jane Garrett called them into the dining room, everyone moved to their chairs around the table. Rachel was directed to sit beside Andrew and to the left of his father. Maura was on his opposite side, with her grandmother at the other end of the table. Directly across from the little girl was her uncle Nate, then Kenna and her uncle Daniel.

"Look at this," Nate said, lowering himself into his chair. "Mom got out the fancy plates—and it's not Thanksgiving, Christmas or Easter."

Jane gave him a narrow-eyed stare as she passed the platter of baked ham to him. "We don't only use the good china on holidays."

"No, but the good china, candles and linen napkins?"

Daniel looked at Andrew across the table. "Why didn't you tell us you were dating royalty?"

Maura's eyes went wide. "Like a princess?"

"A princess is royalty," Andrew confirmed. "But Rachel isn't a princess."

"Oh," the little girl said, obviously disappointed.

"Your uncles, on the other hand, are royal pains in the you-know-what," he said, and made her giggle.

Rachel was smiling, too, as she accepted the bowl of peas from Andrew's father and spooned some onto her plate.

"Now, in a deliberate change of topic," Jane announced, "I was talking to Susan today—"

"My dad's brother Tom's wife," Andrew said to Rachel in an undertone.

"—who heard from Kelly—"

"My cousin Jack's wife."

"—that Lukas and Julie have finally set a date for their wedding, so the invitations should be going out soon."

"Lukas is Jack's brother," he continued his explanations. "They also have another brother, Matt. They're cousins who live in upstate New York."

Across the table, Nathan shook his head. "Three cousins and three weddings within twelve months."

"My friend Kristy's mom is getting married," Maura told her uncle.

"Does she live in Pinehurst?"

The little girl shook her head.

"Nate thinks there's something in the water up there," Andrew explained to Rachel.

His brother shrugged, not denying it. "It's the only logical explanation I could think of for three seemingly rational men choosing to strap on the ball and chain."

Maura frowned. "What ball and chain?"

"It's an expression," her father explained, with a harsh look at Nate. "And not an appropriate one."

"When is the wedding?" Daniel asked.

"The end of June, and I expect all of you—" his mother looked pointedly around the table at each of her sons in turn "—to be there. Matt and Georgia got married so quickly none of us were able to attend, and I understood that everyone couldn't get away for Jack and Kelly's ceremony because they got married on a Wednesday night, but there is no reason for anyone to miss Lukas and Julie's wedding."

"I'll go," Nate assured her. "But I won't drink the water."

"Maybe you could invite your cousins from Pinehurst to come here for a party before then," Jane suggested.

"Mom and Dad's fortieth anniversary is coming up," Andrew explained to Rachel. "And Mom's afraid that if she doesn't remind us every couple of weeks, we might forget."

Rachel agreed that forty years was definitely something to celebrate, and she found herself wishing that she might someday share that kind of long-term commitment with someone. Maybe even the man she was seated beside right now....

Chapter Eleven

"Well, that wasn't so bad," Rachel decided, after they'd said good-night to Andrew's parents and were headed back to her place. Maura was in the backseat, playing a hand-held video game, and although her attention seemed focused on her screen, Rachel kept her voice low so as not to be overheard.

"Were you expecting that it would be?" Andrew asked, amusement evident in his tone.

"I didn't know what to expect," she admitted. "It's been a long time since I went home to meet anyone's parents."

"I bet you it's been a lot longer since I took anyone new home."

She'd suspected as much, and she appreciated that his family had been gracious and welcoming. Well, his parents, anyway. His brothers had gone out of their way to embarrass Andrew, but she'd grown up with a brother who found pleasure in tormenting her at every turn, so she didn't hold it against them.

But she was curious about something. "What's the story with Daniel and Kenna?"

"There's no story," Andrew told her. "They're friends."

"Just friends?"

"Yeah." He glanced over. "Why are you asking?"

She shrugged. "I just thought there were some…undercurrents."

He shook his head. "They've known each other too long and too well."

But Rachel wasn't convinced. There was definitely something more between Andrew's youngest brother and the woman he'd introduced as his best friend, even if neither of them seemed to be aware of it.

Maura didn't usually mind homework. Daddy said it proved that she was a big girl now, so she'd sit up at the island in the kitchen and do her math work sheets or practice her spelling, usually while Sharlene was making dinner. But on Thursdays she had piano lessons right after school, so she didn't get to her homework until after dinner.

She sat at the counter staring at the blank page in front of her and thought about what Mrs. Patterson had asked her to draw. She didn't really like art—especially drawing. She could sometimes picture what she wanted to draw in her head, but it never looked right when she put it down on paper. She'd tried to draw a dog once, and Kristy said it looked like a cow. Mrs. Patterson had scolded Kristy for laughing and said that effort was more important than results.

Maura didn't really care. She knew she was smart. Whenever Mrs. Patterson wanted something read out loud to the class, she usually asked Maura because she could read way above her grade level. At least that's what it said on her report card.

She liked to read. She liked to imagine herself inside

the stories. Right now she was reading the Harry Potter books. Not all by herself, but with her daddy. It was her favorite part of the day. He said it was a tradition that her mom had started when she was just a baby. She couldn't remember reading with her mom, but she looked forward to reading with Daddy every night.

She wished she could be reading instead of doing homework now. And then she wished that she had a magic wand like Harry Potter and could make her paper disappear. But the page and the crayons remained stubbornly there.

Sometimes Mrs. Patterson let them cut pictures out of magazines if they didn't want to draw. She frowned, trying to remember what her teacher had called the kind of picture that was a bunch of pictures put together. But it didn't matter, anyway, because she said everyone had to make a drawing this time.

Most of the time she rushed to finish because it didn't matter if she took her time and tried to be careful—her drawing sucked. But this time she was really going to try. Because she could see it so clearly in her mind, the one thing that she wanted most in the whole world.

Andrew knew that Maura disliked drawing. She was happy enough to color so long as it was a picture in a book, but she became easily frustrated when trying to draw something that didn't look the way she wanted it to. So when she told him that her homework was to draw a picture, he figured she would be finished and packing up her crayons in less than fifteen minutes.

When she was still at the counter more than half an hour later, he went to investigate.

"Mrs. Patterson told us to draw a picture of what we wanted to do for spring break," she told him.

"How's it coming?"

"I think it's okay," she said.

Which was a considerable improvement over the "it sucks" that was her usual response.

"Can I see it?"

She nodded.

He stepped closer and peered over her shoulder. He recognized the basic shape of a castle in the background. Since their trip to Orlando the previous spring, Disney World had been her favorite place in the world.

"Is that one of the Disney princesses?"

"No. It's Rachel."

He could see it now. The long brown hair and the blue eyes, but it was the very round belly that made him break out in a sweat. Not sure he even wanted to ask about that, he opted to state the obvious: "Rachel didn't go to Florida with us."

"I know. But Mrs. Patterson said we could use our imagination to think about what we most wanted. This is what I most want."

"To go back to Disney World?"

"To be a family. You, me, Rachel and a baby brother or sister."

It was her earnest expression as much as the words that tore at his heart. She wasn't asking for much—at least not from her perspective. She only wanted the same thing most of her friends and classmates already had.

But from his perspective, she was asking for the one thing he didn't think he could give her. It wasn't that he'd completely ruled out the possibility of getting married again or having another child—it was that he'd only been dating Rachel for a short while and his little girl was already thinking in terms of happily-ever-after.

"We could be a family if you and Rachel got married," she told him.

"I have no plans to get married again anytime soon," he said gently.

"Why not?" Maura demanded. "Kristy's mom's getting married again, so she's gonna have two dads and I don't even have one mom."

"You had a mother, and she loved you very much." He hated that he had to remind her of the fact, that her own memories were so faded they were almost nonexistent.

"But why can't I have another one?"

He didn't have the first clue how to answer that question. He blew out a breath and looked at her picture again, at the balloon shaped like a Mickey head that the little girl was holding.

"If you had a balloon and it popped or floated away in the sky, I'd be happy to buy you another one," he assured her. "But a person isn't a balloon. A person isn't replaceable. When you lose someone who's important to you, you don't just find someone else to take their place."

"But Kristy's mom—"

"Stop it!" Andrew snapped. "I'm tired of hearing about Kristy's mom."

Maura's chin quivered and her eyes filled with tears.

He scrubbed his hands over his face. "I'm sorry, Maura. I didn't mean to yell at you. I just don't know how to help you understand that the fantasy you're imagining might not happen."

Big, fat tears spilled onto her cheeks. "I'm n-never gonna get a new mom?"

"I'm not saying never," he told her gently. "I'm just saying that you shouldn't get your hopes up right now, because these things don't happen quickly or easily."

"B-but I thought you l-liked Rachel."

Each sob was like a dagger to his heart.

"I do like Rachel," he told her, and it was true. He enjoyed talking to her and being with her, and he really enjoyed making love with her.

But it was still a long way from that to wanting to spend

the rest of his life with her. He'd made that commitment once, because he'd loved Nina completely. And losing her had left an enormous hole in his heart that he didn't think would ever heal.

Being with Rachel had filled up most of that empty space, and he was grateful to her for that. But he wasn't ready to get down on one knee.

"If she's n-not gonna be my n-new mommy, why did you l-let me l-love her?"

Maura crumpled her carefully drawn picture in her fist and threw it to the ground before she raced out of the room, trampling his heart beneath her tiny feet in the process.

Rachel wasn't expecting to hear from Andrew Friday morning. They already had plans to get together that night because he and Maura were leaving Saturday morning to go skiing in Colorado over the little girl's spring break. So when she got his text message, asking if she could meet him for coffee, she wondered if something had come up to change his plans. Or maybe he was going to invite her to go to Aspen with them.

The possibility made her heart bump happily inside her chest. She wouldn't be able to accept, of course. There was no way she could abandon the shop for a whole week, especially with no notice to Holly or Trish or Elaine. But the possibility that he might ask her filled her heart with joy and hope.

Maybe she was jumping the gun a bit—after all, they'd only been dating for a few weeks. On the other hand, he had taken her home to meet his family, and it didn't seem like a huge jump from that to taking a trip together.

But when she walked into the Bean There Café, he didn't look like a man who was excited about his vacation. In fact, he barely looked at her at all. And when their drinks were ready and they sat down, he didn't say anything for several long minutes.

Rachel sipped her hot beverage and tried to ignore the tangling of nerves in her belly. When the silence became unbearable, she finally said, "Whatever it is, please just tell me."

He looked up from his mug. "I think we should cool things down a little bit."

Though she'd scorched her tongue on the latte, she knew he wasn't talking about their drinks. What she didn't know was what had precipitated this decision, why he wanted to cool things down only a few days after taking her home to meet his family.

"I don't understand," she said. "What's changed?"

"It's Maura," he admitted.

"She doesn't want us to be together?" she asked, trying to make sense of his response. Because the little girl had seemed more than happy whenever Rachel spent time with her.

"Actually, it's just the opposite. She's thrilled about our relationship—so thrilled that she's started to fantasize about you becoming her new mother."

And obviously that bothered him. Because he didn't want his daughter to forget the woman who had given birth to her? Because he had no intention of marrying ever again? Or because he didn't think Rachel would be an appropriate mother for his child if he did want to marry again?

She swallowed. "And you don't see our relationship moving in that direction?"

"We've only been together a few weeks," he reminded her.

She just nodded woodenly.

Only a few weeks, and he was dumping her. He could

call it cooling off—he could call it whatever he wanted—but they both knew what it really meant.

"Maura started talking about wanting a new mother before she even met you," he confided. "But now...now she's focused on you. She doesn't just want *a* mother, she wants *you* to be her mother."

"And you just wanted sex without any messy emotional ties," she noted.

He winced. "That's not fair."

"Really? You're going to talk to me about what's fair? Because this is exactly what I wanted to avoid, and your sudden concern about Maura now proves to me that you never really intended to let me be part of your life."

"I did want you to be part of my life," he insisted. "You were the first woman I've met since Nina died that I really wanted to spend time with and get to know better. You made me want to take a chance and risk my heart again... but I didn't realize that I would be risking my daughter's, too."

"What about my heart?" she challenged.

He glanced away. "We knew the risks."

"Yeah, and I knew that getting involved with a man who had a child would be complicated. But you made me want to give you a chance—to give us a chance."

"I really am sorry, Rachel."

She heard the anguish in his tone and knew that this hadn't been an easy decision for him. But that knowledge didn't make her heart ache any less.

"Not half as sorry as I am," she told him, then pushed back her chair and walked out.

Andrew wondered what it said about him that, in the space of less than twenty-four hours, two females had walked out on him.

For the first few days after their talk about Rachel,

Maura's attitude had been chillier than the snow on the slopes in Aspen. Although she'd gradually warmed up to him again, he knew she was still confused.

Now they were home again, and he was staring into a shot of Jack Daniel's at the Bar Down Sports Bar, and wondering how it was that he'd set out to do the right thing, to prevent his daughter from being hurt, and she was hurting, anyway. It was a safe bet that Rachel was still hurting, too. And, if anyone had asked, he'd have to admit it hadn't exactly been a banner week for him, either.

Not that he expected anyone to ask. After all, a guy didn't go into a bar all by himself at four o'clock on a Friday afternoon because he wanted to talk about how completely he'd screwed up his own life. No—he went into that bar because he wanted to get rip-roaring drunk and *forget* how completely he'd screwed up his own life.

Thankfully, Maura was with her grandparents this weekend, so rip-roaring drunk wasn't out of the question.

He lifted the glass to his lips and swallowed the shot. He held the empty glass out for a refill.

Chelsea, the bartender and long ago girlfriend of his youngest brother, eyed him warily. "You driving?"

He shook his head. "I'll give my brother a call to pick me up when I'm done."

"Daniel?" she asked, almost hopefully, as she refilled his glass.

He shrugged. "Or Nate." He tossed back the shot.

Chelsea looked at him and sighed. "You keep up this pace, your brother's going to have to pour you into his car."

"Just one more," he promised.

"Woman trouble?" she asked.

"With a capital *T*."

"Wouldn't it be easier to buy her some flowers and tell her you're sorry?"

"She likes flowers," he agreed.

"And flowers won't hammer on your skull tomorrow morning," Chelsea said helpfully, moving down the bar to serve another customer.

When she came back, she set a mug of black coffee in front of him. He scowled at her, but lifted the mug to his lips.

He didn't remember taking his phone out or talking to his brother, so when Nate settled onto the empty stool beside him, he suspected that Chelsea had made the call.

Nate looked at Andrew, then at the clock, and shook his head. "How long have you been here?"

Andrew squinted at the watch on his wrist, but how was he supposed to read numbers that were moving around? He shook his head. "Don't know."

"Okay. Can you tell me why you're completely tanked at seven o'clock?"

"I miss her."

"Nina?"

"Rachel."

Nate sighed. "You can tell me the sad tale on the way home."

As spring kicked into high gear with wedding season just around the corner, Buds & Blooms got busier, for which Rachel was grateful. She enjoyed the work and she appreciated the fact that it kept her hands and her mind occupied. Of course, the shop didn't keep her busy 24-7, and the nights were long and lonely.

Despite Holly's alternating bribes, threats and pleas, she rarely went out. Although her dating hiatus had officially ended with Andrew, she had no interest in going to bars or clubs to make meaningless conversation with strangers.

On her next Saturday afternoon off, Rachel decided to take her nephews to Buster Bear's Boisterous Bash. Buster's was a restaurant/arcade designed specifically for kids, which meant it was noisy and crowded and, of course, the boys absolutely loved it. Although they liked to run around—and often in different directions—she didn't worry about them because the establishment had a strict policy that no adult was admitted without a child, combined with the further security of invisible hand stamps. The stamps identified all members of a group who arrived together to ensure no child left with the wrong group.

In addition to the main games area, there were several themed party rooms that could be rented out to groups. It was rare for any of the rooms not to be in use, and today was no exception. The disco ball was spinning and music was pumping inside Randy Raccoon's Rock 'n' Roll Room; another group was jumping on trampolines and screaming in the ball pits of Fiona Fox's Fun Zone; while still more kids were embarking on intergalactic adventures in Sammy Squirrel's Space Port. But it was the scene in Penny Penguin's Princess Palace that snagged her attention.

She recognized Andrew first, but then she spotted Maura, too. The little girl was dressed in a sparkly gown with an elaborately bejeweled tiara on her head—clearly designating her as the guest of honor.

The room had been lavishly decorated with streamers and balloons in pale pink and lavender, and there must have been thirty kids in the room. Andrew was slicing the cake while the woman beside him was adding scoops of ice cream to the plates.

It wouldn't have fazed Rachel the least bit if it had been either of Maura's grandmothers helping out at what was obviously the little girl's birthday party. But this woman was a lot younger, standing a lot closer to Andrew than was necessary, and smiling at him in a way that did not suggest any kind of familial relationship.

Looking at her, Rachel felt as if the bottom of her stomach had dropped out. She'd believed him when he'd said that he didn't want Maura to get any ideas about a new mother. And now, only two weeks later, he was with another woman—a woman who obviously felt very comfortable with both the man and his daughter.

"C'mon." Trent tugged on her hand. "We wanna play."

Rachel focused her attention back to her nephews and managed a smile. "Absolutely—that's why we're here."

But she'd lingered outside of the party room for too long, because before they'd taken three steps, Maura spotted her through the window and came racing over.

The little girl threw her arms around Rachel, hugging her tight. "Are you here for my party?"

She looked so happy to see her, and the sparkle in her eyes was so much like her father's, that it made Rachel's heart ache. But that sparkle hadn't been there the last time she'd seen Andrew, when he'd decided it wasn't a good idea to take their relationship any further.

"No, we're just here for some pizza and games," she said. "We didn't know it was your birthday today."

"It's not really my birthday until Tuesday," Maura explained. "But we're having my class party today."

Inside the party room, Andrew was refilling juice cups. The blonde, who had been paying more attention to him than anything else, suddenly seemed to realize that the birthday girl was missing. She looked around frantically for a minute, then spotted her standing just outside the door.

"You can come in for cake, if you want," Maura said to the boys. "Everyone from my class is here."

"Maura." The blonde woman came through the door and put a protective hand on the child's shoulder. "You're missing your party."

"This is my teacher, Mrs. Patterson," Maura told Rachel.

The teacher smiled, but her gaze was cool. "And you are?"

"Rachel Ellis," she said.

"Rachel's my daddy's friend," Maura told her teacher. "And my friend, too."

A revelation that caused the other woman's already-icy gaze to chill even further.

"Maura, why are you… Oh," Andrew's question trailed off when he spotted Rachel in the corridor. "Hi."

"Hi." She wondered if it was possible to feel any more awkward than she did at that moment. She was completely unprepared for this encounter now. She'd dressed comfortably for a day with her nephews in faded jeans and an old hoodie with her hair swept up into a casual ponytail and a bare minimum of makeup. In comparison, Maura's undeniably lovely teacher was wearing a tailored silk blouse and stylish trousers, with her hair perfectly coiffed and her makeup immaculate.

She held up the number they'd been given when they placed their food order, wielding it like a sword that might protect her from the feelings of inadequacy that assailed her from all sides. "We have to, uh, grab a table…before our pizza is ready."

"Pizza!" Trent agreed.

"Play!" Scott countered.

"We have lots of time for both," Rachel promised. But she turned back to Maura and said, "Happy Birthday."

Then she quickly ushered her nephews away before anyone could notice the tears that burned her eyes.

Chapter Twelve

Andrew watched Rachel until she'd rounded the corner and disappeared from his sight, mentally kicking himself for not knowing what to say or do. Maura had already returned to the party room and her friends when Denise Patterson put her hand on his arm.

Her hand lingered, a clear sign of attentiveness that exceeded the usual parent-teacher standards. He didn't know how to telegraph his disinterest any more clearly than he'd already done, and he silently wished that the next half hour would pass quickly so that Maura's party would be over and he could take his daughter home.

"I think the birthday girl is ready to open her presents," Denise said.

He nodded and stepped back, forcing her hand to drop away.

When he'd agreed to Maura's request to invite everyone in her class—because he would have agreed to almost anything to see her smile again—he hadn't expected her to include the teacher. Even more surprising to Andrew was that the teacher had accepted. Considering that Denise Patterson spent six hours a day, five days a week, with the kids, he would have thought that she'd look forward to her weekends away from them. Despite that, she'd been the first to RSVP.

When she'd volunteered to help with the party, he hadn't known how to refuse the gracious offer. And, truthfully, he was grateful to have another adult present.

He hadn't asked his parents because he knew they were busy getting ready for the family party for Maura the following day, and he hadn't invited the Wakefields because he was still annoyed with Carol for being rude to Rachel. Although he had invited both of his brothers, they'd quickly manufactured excuses to explain that they weren't available. He knew they both loved Maura, but apparently they didn't love the prospect of being in a party room with thirty-two other first graders.

Which had left him with only Denise Patterson. Unfortunately, he'd quickly realized that her offer wasn't without strings—and she spent most of the party trying to wrap those strings around him.

By the time Maura's classmates had all been picked up and he'd finally extricated himself from Mrs. Patterson and loaded Maura's presents into the trunk of his car, he was exhausted. Three hours at Buster Bear's Boisterous Bash was more than any adult should be forced to endure and yet, when Maura asked if she could play a few more games, he found himself buying her another cup of tokens.

Then he bought two cups of coffee and went in search of Rachel.

He found her in a booth near the arcade section. She was alone now, with the remnants of a pepperoni pizza on a tray in front of her. There was something about her—he didn't know if it was her blue eyes or the easy smile or distinctly feminine curves, but something definitely got to him.

He still wanted her. There was no denying that simple fact. He wanted her naked in his bed, those long, slender limbs wrapped around him as she panted his name. Unfortunately, he was pretty sure he'd destroyed any possibility of that ever happening again.

He'd been the one to pursue her, to convince her to give them a chance when she'd clearly been reluctant to do so. And then, when she was starting to believe they could have something together, he'd told her it was over.

He watched her stack the used cups and plates and wondered if he should just let her be.

He wasn't in the habit of second-guessing himself, but he'd been doing a lot of exactly that since he'd said goodbye to her two weeks earlier. He worried that what he wanted might not be what was best for Maura; and he worried that he was using his daughter as an excuse to avoid getting too deeply involved with a woman who had somehow already taken hold of his heart.

It never ceased to amaze Rachel how quickly two little boys could annihilate the better part of a pepperoni pizza. When Scott and Trent had devoured their fill of the pie and gulped down their sodas, she sent them to wash up before letting them loose in the arcade with their tokens. When they were gone, she was left alone with her thoughts and a cold slice of untouched pizza on her plate—both of which were equally unappealing.

She should have anticipated that she might bump into Andrew sometime. In a town the size of Charisma, it was probable if not inevitable. If she'd been at Valentino's or the movie theater, she might have been prepared. But today was supposed to be about her nephews and fun—and forgetting that her heart had been bruised.

But then, as if she'd somehow managed to conjure him from her thoughts, Andrew was sliding into the opposite seat. He set a cup of coffee on the table in front of her.

She didn't want the coffee, and she definitely didn't want to sit across the table from him as if they were friendly acquaintances taking advantage of the fact their paths had crossed to share a drink and conversation.

But she reached for the caddy on the table and took out a couple of packets of sugar and nondairy creamer because it gave her something to focus on other than him. "Where's Maura?" she asked.

"Dancing her way to stardom—or at least prize tickets."

And though she'd promised she wouldn't ask, she heard herself say, "Is Mrs. Patterson with her?"

"No. Mrs. Patterson left with the rest of the birthday guests." He reached across the table and touched her hand, forcing her to look at him. "I didn't invite her to come here today—Maura did."

She tugged her hand away to stir her coffee. "Why are you telling me?"

"Because I didn't want you to get the wrong idea."

"I don't have any ideas," she assured him.

"I've missed you, Rachel."

They were words, easily spoken, and not any reason for her heart to give a traitorous bump. But it bumped anyway, forcing her to remind it that he wouldn't have reason to miss her if he hadn't dumped her.

"You were the one who ended it," she reminded him.

"I didn't know what to do," he admitted. "I was worried about Maura—"

"You made that clear."

"Did I? Because nothing was clear to me—then or now."

"So what do you want, Andrew?"

"I just want to talk to you."

"This isn't the time or the place."

He nodded. "Okay. I'll come over later."

She shook her head. "Scott and Trent are sleeping over at my place tonight." And she was grateful for that, because she needed time to shore up the defenses around her heart that had been weakened by only five minutes in his company.

"Tomorrow?" he suggested.

"I'm working all day."

"Tomorrow night?"

"I have plans."

He sighed. "You're not going to make this easy for me, are you?"

"Make what easy?" she challenged. "What do you really want?

"Do you want me to tell you that it's okay that you made me believe you wanted me in your life before you banished me from it? Or that you took me home to meet your family so I could decide I really liked them before I found out I wasn't ever going to see them again? Or maybe I'm supposed to forgive you for letting me almost fall in love with you and then making it clear that you don't feel the same way?"

"Maybe I do feel the same way," he finally said. "And maybe that's what scared me so much."

She slid out of the booth. "*Maybe* isn't good enough."

He took the hint. He didn't call her the next day; he didn't stop by her apartment or drop in at Buds & Blooms. Apparently he was going to let her have the last word, and while it had felt pretty good in the moment to pour out all of the feelings that she'd been holding inside, now that she'd done so, Rachel only felt empty.

Thankfully she did have plans the next night—a casual get-together with Holly and some other friends from high school, including the recently engaged Amy Jensen, Amy's newlywed sister Lisa Seabrook, and Jennifer James—known to her friends and clients as JJ. And while Rachel enjoyed hanging out with her friends, munching on nachos and drinking margaritas, her mind kept drifting, wondering what Andrew and Maura were doing and wishing things had turned out differently for all of them.

Monday night she finally kept her long-forgotten date with Eve and Roarke, staying up well past her usual bedtime to make sure the bad guys got their due. Tuesday started early, with the usual 7:00 a.m. delivery, then there were a few consults for flowers for an engagement party, a baby shower and an awards banquet. By the afternoon, she was feeling pretty confident that she would eventually forget about Andrew Garrett—and then he walked into the shop, and her heart nearly leaped out of her chest.

"Before you tell me this isn't the time or place—I'm here to buy flowers."

"Maura's birthday," she remembered.

He nodded. "She got such a kick out of being here the day that you put together the bouquet for my mom, I thought she'd like some flowers of her own."

"A bouquet or an arrangement?"

"What's the difference?"

"Essentially whether the flowers are wrapped in paper or presented in a vase or other container."

"I guess an arrangement."

She gestured to the refrigerated display case. "Did you want to look for something in there or did you have specific flowers in mind?"

He examined the arrangements through the glass. "Pink," he said. "I want something more pink."

"Why don't you pick out a vase and I'll get some flowers together?"

He selected a tall frosted cylinder, and Rachel filled it with pink roses, gerberas and hypericum.

"She'll love that," he said, and set his credit card on the counter.

She slid it back to him. "Tell Maura happy birthday from me."

"You could tell her yourself."

She wished she could. She missed the little girl as much as she'd missed Andrew, but if she saw her again, it would only rip the scab off a wound that had barely begun to heal. "I can't turn my emotions on and off like you do, Andrew."

"Do you think it was easy for me to let you go? Do you think a single day has gone by in the past two-and-a-half weeks that I didn't think about you first thing in the morning and wish you were beside me when I went to bed at night?"

"I wouldn't know." But it was a lie—she could see the truth in his eyes. But she also knew it didn't change anything.

"You were right," he said to her. "I had no business asking you to give me a second chance when I wasn't ready to put my feelings on the line. So here it is—I love you, Rachel."

They were the words she never thought she'd hear him say, and though they filled her heart, she was wary.

"Do you want me to say it again?" he asked when she remained silent. "Because I'll say it a thousand times if you want—I love you, I love you, I love you. Do you want me to go on?"

Her eyes filled with tears. "Why are you doing this?"

"Because I love you."

She shook her head. "I can't keep putting my heart on the line and having it shoved back at me."

"I didn't mean to hurt you."

"I know you were thinking about Maura," she told him. "I get that. But that didn't make it any easier."

"This is all new territory for me. I didn't expect things to move so fast, and I panicked."

"And how do I know you won't panic again?"

"Because I've had more than two weeks to see what my life is like without you in it, and it wasn't fun.

"I miss you, Rachel… Maura misses you, too."

She was grateful when the door chimed as another customer entered the shop.

She saw regret and resignation in his eyes when Andrew picked up the vase of flowers. "We're going out for dinner tonight—six o'clock at Valentino's. I know Maura would love it if you came, too."

Rachel shook her head, her throat too tight to speak.

"We'll get a table for three," he told her. "Just in case you change your mind."

She changed her mind more than a dozen times before the end of the day.

"I shouldn't go."

Holly looked up from the stems she was clipping. "Are you asking me or telling me?"

"I don't know," Rachel admitted.

"Because I agree that you probably shouldn't, but I know you will, anyway."

She frowned. "How can you know when I haven't even decided yet?"

"I know because I know you," Holly said. "And I know you're head over heels for both the man and his daughter."

It was futile to deny it, and if she tried, Holly would see right through her. She sighed. "You warned me not to fall in love."

"Yeah, but since when do you ever listen to me?" Holly dried her hands and shoved Rachel toward the door. "Go. I'll lock up tonight."

Rachel detoured past Buy The Book on her way home

to pick up a gift for Maura. Phoebe was sitting at a stool working the cash while Kinsley shelved new stock. Rachel found what she wanted right away, and Phoebe chatted casually with her as she processed the sale and gift-wrapped her purchase. Rachel expected her to ask who the book was for, but she didn't. She did, however, squeeze Rachel's hand as she passed over the bag.

"I'm glad you're following your heart."

Rachel didn't know if she felt better having Phoebe's blessing, but she knew there was no turning back.

At her apartment, she changed her clothes and touched up her makeup, then headed out to Valentino's.

"I knew you were the third," Gemma said to Rachel as soon as she walked in. "When Andrew asked for a table for three, I knew you would be joining them."

"Don't read too much into this," Rachel warned her friend.

The hostess waved a hand dismissively. "Every time I peek into the dining room, the man is looking at the entrance, waiting for you to walk through it."

As if Rachel wasn't already nervous enough.

"Maybe this isn't a good idea."

Gemma gave her a nudge toward the wide arched doorway. "The pizza Maura wanted should be coming out soon, so you better get in there."

Rachel took a deep breath and stepped into the dining room.

She spotted him immediately, and her traitorous heart did a happy dance inside of her chest. Whether he'd been watching the door or just happened to glance up when she walked through it, he saw her at the same time. And the smile that curved his lips had her already-dancing heart stepping up the pace.

She didn't want to get ahead of herself, to expect

too much. She was only here because it was Maura's birthday....

Follow your heart.

As she heard the echo of Phoebe's urging in the back of her mind, she acknowledged that she was also here because her heart wouldn't let her be anywhere else.

Maura had been sitting across from her father with her back to the entrance, but she turned now, and the smile that spread across her face went a long way toward healing Rachel's bruised emotions. Then she slid out of her chair to wrap her arms around Rachel and hug her tight. "I'm so glad you came."

"Me, too," she said, and meant it. "Happy Birthday, Maura."

The little girl accepted the brightly wrapped package. "Can I open it?"

"It is your birthday, isn't it?"

Andrew had stood up, too, and he pulled back Rachel's chair for her to sit. "Thank you," he whispered, close to her ear, as she lowered herself into the chair.

She didn't know what to say and wasn't sure she wouldn't end up regretting the decision to come here, so she just nodded.

Maura climbed back onto her chair and tore at the paper that covered her gift. "Daddy—look. It's the second Harry Potter book."

"I thought you must be getting close to the end of the first one."

"Just six more chapters," Maura told her. "Daddy said he would take me to the bookstore to get the next one when we were done, but now he doesn't have to."

When the pizza came out, it had Happy Birthday spelled out in green pepper and a smiley face made out of pepperoni in the middle. Of course, when Maura saw that, she didn't want to eat it, so Andrew took out his cell phone to snap a photo of it for her.

After the pizza had been devoured, there was cake for the birthday girl. Andrew and Rachel both declined dessert but had coffee while Maura enjoyed her chocolate truffle cake.

"Did you have a good birthday?" Rachel asked as they were leaving the restaurant.

"I had four birthdays," the little girl told her, and proceeded to count them out on her fingers. "One at Buster Bear's, one with Grandma Carol and Grandpa Ed, a big party at Grandma Jane and Grandpa Dave's house, with all my aunts and uncles and cousins, and then tonight."

"You're a lucky girl."

Maura nodded. "But I liked this one best, 'cuz it had you."

Andrew knew that he was lucky to be given a second chance with Rachel, and he wasn't about to blow it. He'd put his heart on the line and told her how he felt, but she'd remained closemouthed about her own feelings. And he told himself that was okay. Right now, he should just enjoy being with her and not push for more than she was ready to give.

But he talked to her every day, sometimes more than once a day, and he saw her as often as he could. And slowly, over the next several days, her resistance began to melt. She let him hold her hand in the dark of the movie theater, and kiss her good-night if Maura was already tucked into bed. He really liked kissing her. He liked doing a lot of other things with her, too, but he reminded himself that he was trying to take things slower this time.

And then, on the Friday night ten days after Maura's birthday, she was invited to a sleepover at Kristy's house. He decided to invite Rachel to his place for dinner, deliberately neglecting to mention that his daughter wouldn't be there.

Of course, the first question she asked when she arrived was, "Where's Maura?"

"At Kristy's."

She looked at him, obviously waiting for an explanation.

"I didn't tell you because I was afraid you might not come if you knew," he admitted. "Not that I invited you with the expectation of anything more than sharing a meal and some time alone with you."

She seemed to consider his response for a minute before she asked, "What's for dinner?"

"I have potatoes baking in the oven, a green salad in the fridge, and steaks ready to go on the grill."

"You're actually cooking?"

"Grilling," he clarified.

She smiled as she stepped out of her shoes, and he exhaled a quiet sigh of relief at the realization that she was going to stay.

He took her hands and gently drew her toward him. She didn't resist. Not even when he slipped his arms around her waist and lowered his head to kiss her. And the way she kissed him back gave him hope that she may have finally, truly, forgiven him.

"I've really missed you." He whispered the words against her lips.

"I missed you, too," she admitted.

He wanted to ask her to stay the night, but he'd promised her that he didn't have any expectations—and it was true. But he was desperately holding on to hope that she'd forgiven him sufficiently to get naked with him again.

Instead he said, "I should start the barbecue and get those steaks on."

"I don't mind eating later."

"How much later?"

"After," she told him, and brought his mouth down to hers again.

He swept her into his arms and carried her upstairs to his bed.

Chapter Thirteen

There was another fireplace in his bedroom.

Of course, Rachel hadn't noticed it when he first carried her into the master suite. She hadn't been aware of anything but the massive bed in the center of the room and the man who lowered her onto it.

But now that her body was sated and her heart rate was almost back to normal, she took a minute to look around.

The mission-style furniture had strong, masculine lines that suited the man and the room. The walls were taupe, the hardwood floors had an espresso finish, and she suspected the sheets tangled around her were the finest Egyptian cotton.

"I bet this room could be the feature spread in a home-decorating magazine."

He grinned. "Right now, with you sprawled naked on my bed, I'm thinking it looks like a different kind of magazine spread."

She picked up one of the pillows and swung it at him.

He caught the pillow—and her—and in one quick move, pinned her beneath him. He looked into her eyes, and his expression turned serious. "Are we okay?"

Her brows lifted. "I'd say that what just happened here is a few notches up the scale from okay."

"What just happened here was off the scale," he told her. "But you know that's not what I'm asking."

She nodded.

"Yes, you know, or yes, we're okay?"

"Both."

He lowered his head to kiss her gently then drew back when her stomach growled hungrily.

"I guess it's later," he acknowledged.

He opened a bottle of pinot noir to accompany their meal and poured two glasses. When he went outside to grill the steaks, she took her glass of wine to keep him company.

He'd told her that he'd hired Sharlene because he couldn't cook. Rachel didn't know how true that was, but when she took her first bite of the steak, she knew that he could grill. The baked potatoes were a little overcooked, because neither of them had thought to take them out of the oven before they went upstairs, but she didn't mind. And Andrew covered his with sour cream and chives and grated cheese and crumbled bacon so that he probably didn't even realize it.

When the meal was finished, she pushed back her chair and rose from the table.

"Where are you going?" he asked her.

"To clear the table."

"Leave it for later."

Her brows lifted. "Later?"

He grinned and tugged her hand, so that she tumbled onto his lap. "I've got a lot of time to make up for."

"It doesn't all have to be in one night," she told him.

"I know." He nuzzled her throat, and the rasp of stubble

on her tender skin made her shiver. "I want to make love with you again."

She wanted that, too. Because when she was with Andrew, she felt as if they really were making love.

And she did love him, but she hadn't yet been able to say the words. She didn't know what was holding her back. She didn't think she was punishing him for hurting her—at least not consciously. But for some reason, she felt compelled to keep the depth of her feelings to herself. It was as if she'd given him so much of her heart and herself that she was afraid if she gave him the words, she wouldn't have anything left.

Maura liked having sleepovers at Kristy's house, because Kristy's mom let them stay up really late and she didn't care what they ate. She said that sleepovers were all about pigging out and *not* sleeping. But now that she was really tired, Maura didn't think the buttered popcorn and ice cream with chocolate sauce and an entire bag of gummy bears had been such a good idea.

Or maybe it was the zombie movie they'd watched that was keeping her awake.

She couldn't see her friend in the dark, so she whispered. "Kristy?"

"Yeah?"

"Are zombies real?"

"I don't think so."

"Are you scared?"

"Nuh-uh. We're in the attic—if anyone comes in, they'll get Tiffany first."

Maura didn't find that thought very reassuring.

"Besides, Greg's here. He'd protect us."

That made her feel better. Greg was almost Kristy's daddy, and Maura always felt safe when her daddy was around.

Still, she snuggled a little deeper in the mattress and pulled the covers up a little higher.

"So what's going on with your dad and his girlfriend?" Kristy asked.

"What do you mean?"

"Are they together or broken up?"

"They're together again," she said, happy that it was true.

"Are they gonna get married?"

"I don't know."

"My mom's getting married next month."

Maura nodded, because it was practically all her friend talked about.

"My dad got married, too."

"When?"

"A couple years ago."

Maura was surprised 'cuz Kristy didn't talk much about her dad.

"And now I've got a baby brother," Kristy told her.

"Wow. You're really lucky."

"He's fat and cries a lot."

She didn't know what to say to that.

"And now my dad never comes to see me," Kristy said. "'Cuz he's too busy with the baby."

"Oh."

"Tiffany says it's not the baby's fault…it's my stepmonster's—that's what she calls my stepmother."

"Why?"

"'Cuz she's mean."

"I thought you liked her."

"That was before she married my dad." Kristy yawned. "I'm going to sleep now."

"Okay." Maura rolled over, trying to get more comfortable, but the popcorn, ice cream and gummy bears felt like a hard lump in her belly.

* * *

Being a single father with a young daughter meant that Andrew had to be circumspect in his behavior. Rachel stayed over the night that Maura was at Kristy's, but they both knew that waking up together was going to be the exception rather than the rule.

So he found himself looking forward to the first weekend in May, when his daughter would be with her maternal grandparents and he could have two nights with Rachel.

But on the Monday before that weekend, he got called out of town on business. Work-related emergencies were one of the reasons he'd hired Sharlene. Although she wasn't technically a live-in housekeeper, she had indicated a willingness to work flexible hours—arriving early and staying late and even spending the night, as required. Unfortunately this emergency meeting happened to be called when his housekeeper was in Cleveland because her son's wife had just given birth to Sharlene's first grandbaby.

He was fortunate in that he had a couple of other options. He knew that Maura could stay with either set of grandparents and both would be thrilled to have her. Instead, he decided to ask Rachel to stay with her so that his daughter could remain at home.

Rachel seemed surprised by his request, and a little hesitant. He understood that she had her own life, but he wanted to know that they could figure out a way to merge their respective responsibilities and make it work. And, in the end, she agreed.

Andrew didn't really mind the meetings. They'd never been his favorite part of the job, but he understood that they were an essential aspect of it. What he minded was being away from Maura, and whenever he had to be gone overnight, he always made sure to talk to her before she went to bed. But this time, he was missing Rachel, too.

He'd told her that she could sleep in his bed, because

he liked to think of her tucked between his sheets, preferably naked. But she'd opted for the spare bedroom beside Maura's, insisting that it wouldn't be any less weird for his daughter to find Rachel in his bed just because he wasn't in it.

She was probably right, and he was looking forward to the day when, instead of being something out of the ordinary, it would be the norm for all of them.

Rachel had worried that she wouldn't be able to mesh the demands of her job with the needs of Andrew's daughter. But she found with a little extra planning and some juggling of schedules, it wasn't all that difficult.

Andrew got Maura off to school Monday morning before he left, so Rachel only had to make sure she was at the house when the little girl got off the bus at 3:50 p.m. In the mornings, she was picked up at eight-twenty, so Rachel would have plenty of time to get to the shop before nine and open as usual. Tuesday was a bit trickier, because of the delivery that came at seven, but Holly agreed—with minimal grumbling—to be on hand for that.

After the first twenty-four hours, Rachel started to believe that she could actually do this.

The one snag came at dinnertime on Tuesday. Rachel had gone through the cupboards and found everything she needed to make chicken cacciatore for dinner—but she forgot to take the package of chicken out of the freezer. As a result, they ended up eating grilled cheese, with a side of green beans to ensure that Maura got her daily quotient of vegetables. Because despite the little girl's determined efforts, she did not succeed in convincing Rachel that ketchup was a vegetable.

She was just finishing up her sandwich when Carol Wakefield walked in.

Her entry wasn't preceded by a knock or the bell, she

just came right in. Obviously Andrew's former mother-in-law had a key, because Rachel knew she'd locked the door. Maybe this was Forrest Hill, but she lived downtown and old habits were hard to break.

"Hi, Grandma," Maura said, dunking her last triangle of sandwich into her ketchup.

Carol scowled at her plate. "What's this?"

"We're having dinner," Rachel said, reassuring herself that there was nothing unhealthy about grilled cheese sandwiches.

The older woman ignored Rachel's response to focus on her granddaughter. "Where's your daddy?" she demanded.

"Baltimore?" She looked to Rachel, who nodded in confirmation.

"Where's Sharlene?"

"Ohio." Rachel answered this question when Maura only shrugged.

"Are you telling me that Andrew left my granddaughter in your care?"

She bit back the pithy reply that sprang to her lips and forced a smile. "And we're having a good time, aren't we, Maura?"

"The best," she confirmed.

"I'm sorry," Carol said, not sounding sorry at all. "But this situation is completely unacceptable."

"What situation is that?" a familiar male voice asked from behind her.

"Daddy!" Maura's enthusiastic greeting saved Carol from having to respond.

He caught the little girl in his arms and hugged her tight. She pulled back and noisily kissed each of his cheeks.

"I missed you, baby," he told her.

"I missed you, too, Daddy, but Rachel and I made cookies and painted our toenails and she taught me how to

French braid—but I can't do my own hair so good—and we're up to chapter five in the second Harry Potter book!"

"Chapter five already? Doesn't sound like you had much time to miss me," he noted with a wry grin.

"I had fun with Rachel."

"I knew you would." He shifted his daughter in his arms to face his former mother-in-law. "Was there a reason you stopped by?"

"I wanted to talk to you about our weekend plans with Maura."

If Carol had really wanted to talk about weekend plans, she would have called. The fact that she'd stopped by led him to believe that she'd done so impulsively upon seeing Rachel's car in the driveway and the absence of his own.

"What about them?" he asked mildly.

"Since Maura doesn't have school on Friday, Ed and I have decided to take her to the beach," she said, referring to their house in South Carolina, about a three-and-a-half-hour drive from Charisma. "She loves it there, and the Emmersons are going for the weekend, too, so she'll have other kids to play with."

"That's Steffy and Cody," he reminded Maura.

"Yay!"

He smiled. "Apparently she's good with that plan."

"You're welcome to join us," Carol said to him.

Maura clapped her hands together. "Say yes, Daddy. I want you to come to the beach with us. You, too, Rachel. We can look for seashells and—"

"I'm sorry, Maura," Carol interjected. "But we don't have an extra bedroom for Daddy's…friend."

Maura frowned, and he could see her mentally counting the number of empty bedrooms in the Wakefields' beach house.

"I appreciate the invitation," he said. "But there's a lot

going on at work right now that I'll have to catch up on after being away the last couple of days."

Carol looked as if she wanted to say something more, but then she nodded. "We'll pick Maura up after school on Thursday."

"I'll make sure she's packed," he promised.

"I'm gonna start packing now," Maura said, and raced off to her room.

"She hates me," Rachel said when Carol had gone.

"She wouldn't like anyone who she perceived as taking her daughter's place," Andrew told her.

She understood that—she just wished the other woman felt differently. After all, she was Maura's grandmother, and since Rachel was hoping to spend a lot of time with the little girl, she didn't want to be in constant conflict with the older woman.

"But *I* like you," he said, and wrapped his arms around her. "And I missed you." He brushed his lips against hers. "Did you miss me?"

"Maura kept me so busy, I didn't even realize you were gone," she teased.

His mouth skimmed over her jaw.

"You didn't miss me—"

Down her throat.

"—even a little?"

She swallowed. "Maybe…a little."

He nibbled on her collarbone.

"Maybe—" her breath caught "—a lot."

"Maybe's not good enough," he reminded her.

"Maybe I'll show you how much I missed you after Maura's asleep."

"That's a *maybe* I'll take."

After Maura was asleep and Rachel had very thoroughly assured Andrew that he'd been missed, she slid out of his bed and began gathering her clothes.

"I wish you'd stay," he said, although he knew she wouldn't be persuaded.

"I wish I could," she admitted. "But I need to get home."

"You've slept here the past two nights," he reminded her.

"That's different."

"Why?"

She leaned over the bed to kiss him. "Because you weren't here."

He caught her hand as she reached to put something on the bedside table. "What's that?"

"Your key."

He folded her fingers around it again. "Keep it."

She hesitated. The gesture had been impulsive, but they both knew it wasn't meaningless. "Are you sure?"

"Yeah. In case you're ever overcome with lust and want to crawl into my bed in the middle of the night."

"Or in case you don't want to get out of your nice comfy bed to lock the door behind me when I sneak out in the middle of the night," she teased.

"That works, too," he said, but he got out of bed to say goodbye to her at the door, anyway.

"You gave her a key?"

"Yes, I gave her a key," Andrew repeated, mentally chastising himself for somehow letting that fact slip into a conversation with his brother. "Not a diamond."

"It's practically the same thing," Nate insisted.

"Hardly," he denied. "Although I did spend some time looking at engagement rings when I was in Maryland."

"Wow. You really are in love with her, aren't you?"

"She's the one," he confirmed.

Maybe he'd panicked when Maura had first started talking about wanting a new mommy, but the more time he spent with Rachel, the more he realized that she was exactly what both he and his daughter needed. She was the final piece of the puzzle to make them a family again.

His brother shook his head, and Andrew braced himself for some more of the usual ribbing. Instead, Nate said, "How is it that you've managed to fall in love not once but twice, and I've never even lost my footing?"

He was surprised by the almost-wistful tone in his brother's voice. "Either you've always been careful to watch your step or you've just never met the right woman."

"That's what I used to say—but lately I've been wondering if I was so determined to keep things light and carefree that maybe I did meet her—maybe I met a lot of women, any one of whom might have been the right woman—but I refused to see it."

"What's put you in such a philosophical mood?"

He shrugged. "I guess I've just been thinking about some things since I broke up with Mallory."

"Since she dumped you, you mean?" He couldn't resist teasing.

"Yeah," Nate admitted.

Andrew frowned, surprised by the flatness of his brother's tone. "Were you in love with her?"

"No, but I thought we were building a relationship. It was a bit of a shock to realize that she only wanted no-strings sex."

"Isn't that your ideal woman?"

"Maybe a few years ago. But lately…I kind of like the idea of sharing more than just my bed with a woman."

Andrew's gaze narrowed. "Who are you and what have you done with my brother?"

Nate chuckled. "Is that really so unbelievable?"

"Coming from the guy who taught my daughter the expression 'ball and chain,' yes, it is."

As much as she loved Maura and enjoyed being with her, Rachel couldn't deny that she was looking forward to the weekend and some time alone with Andrew. Unfortunately, she had the late shift at Buds & Blooms on Saturday, so while she got to sleep in a little and wake up in Andrew's arms, her fantasy of staying in bed with him all day had to be put on hold.

But when she got back to his house Saturday afternoon and tracked him down in his workshop, she was treated to a different fantasy in the form of a slightly sweaty, intensely focused and very sexy carpenter. She didn't know what he was doing, but he was wearing an old pair of jeans that had gone white at the stress points and a T-shirt that clung to the delicious muscles of his shoulders and chest. The smell of sawdust filled the air and classic rock pounded in the background as he moved some kind of instrument in long, firm strokes over the surface of the wood. Watching him work, she couldn't help but think about how those same hands now stroking the wood had stroked her body.

She stood in the doorway for several long minutes, mesmerized by the image he presented, enthralled by the bunch and flex of the muscles in his arms, aroused by the bold confidence of his movements.

He looked so primitive and male, and every female part of her instinctively responded. And maybe her pheromones did call to his, because suddenly his head came up and his lips curved in a slow and sexy smile. He wiped the light sheen of perspiration off his brow with the back of his hand as he glanced at the clock. "I thought you had to work until five."

"Trish said that she would stay." She looked around. "Why didn't I get to see this—" she didn't know what it was—a garage or workshop or a combination of both "—when you gave me the grand tour?"

He wiped his hands on a rag. "I didn't think you'd be interested."

And if he'd asked, she probably would have said she

wasn't. But seeing him here, clearly in his milieu, had definitely changed her mind.

"What are you doing?"

"Planing a door for a multimedia cabinet."

"Your own design?"

He nodded. "A lot of furniture design is done by computer today, but I still like to build a prototype from the plans, to ensure no steps or materials were missed. And I like to work with my hands."

"Now I understand the calluses."

He winced. "I sometimes forget how rough my hands are."

"Don't apologize. I love how they feel on me."

He settled those strong, work-roughened hands on her hips. "Yeah?"

"Yeah." He smelled of sawdust and sweat—a surprisingly arousing combination. She lifted her hands to link them behind his head and brought his mouth down to hers for a long kiss.

"I picked up Chinese food for dinner," she said, easing away from him. "It's in the oven, keeping warm for whenever you're ready."

He pulled her back into his arms. "I'm always ready."

The sexy promise in his smile made her heart knock against her ribs.

"I meant for dinner," she clarified. "I don't want to interrupt your work."

"I can't imagine a better interruption," he said, pushing her skirt up over her hips and lifting her onto the workbench.

"Andrew." She'd intended to protest, but his name came out on a breathy sigh that sounded more like a plea.

"Rachel," he responded, a teasing glint in his eyes.

Her breath caught in her throat as he worked her panties over her hips and down her legs.

Then he caught her bottom lip between his teeth and tugged gently. "I want you," he told her. "It doesn't seem to matter how often I have you—it's never enough."

She understood what he was saying. She wanted him, too. It didn't take much—a lingering kiss…a casual touch…sometimes just a heated look—to make her heart race and start her blood pounding. Even now, she could tell by the throbbing between her thighs that she was ready for him.

He continued to nibble on her mouth while she tugged his T-shirt out of his pants, sliding her hands beneath it to trace the rippled contours of his abdomen. His fingertips skimmed up her thighs, teasingly close to her center. She unfastened his belt, then popped the button at the front of his pants and reached inside. Her fingers wrapped around the long, hard length of him, stroked him slowly.

He groaned in appreciation. "We should go inside. Up to the bedroom."

She shook her head. "Here. Take me here. Now."

His hands gripped the wooden edge of the bench as he fought for control. "I don't keep a stash of condoms in my toolbox."

She grabbed the handle of her purse and tugged it toward her, then dumped the contents onto the bench and rifled through them. Wallet, gum, loose change. She finally located the square packet and held it up triumphantly.

"I'm impressed."

She grinned as she tore open the packet. He caught her mouth again in a slow, deep kiss as she unrolled the latex over him. Then he was lifting her off the bench, and easing into her, filling and fulfilling her. She hooked her legs around his waist, anchoring him to her.

"Are you okay?"

The bench was hard and cold and she would probably end up with splinters in her butt, but right now she wasn't thinking about any of that. She wasn't thinking about anything but how good it felt to have him buried deep inside of her. "I'm okay," she assured him.

He began to move as her eyes closed on a sigh of pure pleasure and her fingers dug into his shoulders. She didn't know if it was the angle of their bodies or the novelty of doing it in his workroom, but the pleasure was almost more than she could bear.

As he continued to thrust, harder and deeper, her head fell back and rapped against the pegboard wall covered with instruments and tools of various descriptions. Something fell off and clattered to the ground. Then several other somethings. Crash. Clatter. Clang.

Andrew didn't seem to notice—or maybe he didn't care. Even she registered the sound as if it was faraway. The only thing that mattered in the here and now was Andrew and the indescribable pleasure he gave her whenever she was in his arms.

She'd never experienced anything like this. It wasn't just primitive—it was a little rough and a lot wild, and the orgasm that racked her body left her completely breathless and spent.

Her hand slid off his shoulder to his chest, and she could feel the thunderous pounding of his heart beneath her palm, its rhythm as hard and fast as her own.

He reached up and sifted his fingers through her hair, looking for a bump. "How's the head?"

She laughed softly. "I think I'll live. And if not, I'll die with a smile on my face."

He was smiling, too, when he touched his lips to hers. "I don't know that this bench is tested to withstand that kind of vigorous activity, but I'd be happy to write a product recommendation."

Her head dropped forward to settle against his shoulder

as she tried to catch her breath. "You know what you said about not keeping condoms in your toolbox?"

"Yeah."

"You might want to reconsider."

He chuckled. "Let's go get that Chinese food."

Chapter Fourteen

Maura couldn't sleep.

She could hear Grandpa Ed snoring across the hall, but she knew that wasn't why she was awake. She couldn't sleep because her tummy hurt deep inside and she wanted to go home to Daddy.

He'd called to talk to her after dinner, like he always did. She didn't talk to Rachel, but she knew she was there, because she said "hi" in the background.

Grandma wasn't happy when Maura told her that Rachel was at home with her daddy. She didn't say that she wasn't happy, but Maura could tell because her face got that pinched look.

Before bed, Maura wanted to read Harry Potter but Grandma said it wasn't an appropriate story for a child her age. Instead, she got out a book of fairy tales and read her the story of Cinderella—as if she hadn't heard that enough times since kindergarten.

But listening to Grandma read it, Maura picked up on

some details she hadn't before—like the fact that Cinderella's stepmother was nice to her own children but not to Cinderella. She was a stepmonster, like the woman who married Kristy's dad, and it made Maura wonder if Rachel would get mean, too, if she married Daddy.

Then there was the story about Snow White. She was sent away by the evil queen who married her daddy. And Hansel and Gretel's stepmother told their daddy to abandon them in the woods. Maura knew the stories weren't any more real than Harry Potter, but she wasn't going to take any chances.

She wasn't going to let Rachel marry her daddy.

Sunday morning, Andrew was lured into the kitchen by the tantalizing scents of cooked bacon, fresh coffee and cinnamon. What he saw in the kitchen was even more tempting than what he smelled. Rachel was standing at the stove, dressed in one of his shirts. The sleeves were rolled up past her elbows and the tail fell just past the delectable curve of her bottom.

She was humming quietly to herself as she fried bread in a pan.

"I sometimes wonder if you're with me for my body or my appliances," he said.

She turned to him with a smile. "I assure you I'm appreciative of both."

He took a mug from the cupboard and filled it from the coffeepot.

"I was going to bring you breakfast in bed," she told him.

"And what did I do to deserve that special treatment?"

"Me," she said cheekily.

He chuckled and drew her close for a kiss. "Anytime," he assured her. "In fact—"

"No." She stepped out of his arms. "I'm not going to ruin this French toast."

He looked in the pan. "That doesn't look like normal French toast."

"It's banana cinnamon French toast—I'm expanding your culinary horizons."

"Looks…interesting."

"You'll like it," she promised.

And he did.

But what he liked most was getting creative with the leftover maple syrup, drizzling it over select parts of her body and slowly licking it off. By the time he was done, they were both sticky, so he carried her up to his shower and soaped up every inch of her body. And he really liked that she returned the favor.

Rachel was torn between relief and regret when she went back to her own apartment Sunday night. Every minute that she'd spent with Andrew over the weekend had been incredible, but she knew that she was falling deeper and deeper in love each day. And not just with Andrew, but with his daughter, too.

She'd expected her life to follow a traditional path wherein she'd meet someone special, they'd fall in love, get married and raise a family together. Andrew had already done that whole routine, and, for the past three years, he'd been raising his daughter on his own. He had help from his family, of course, and from Maura's maternal grandparents, but he had ultimate responsibility and made all decisions with respect to this little girl.

Rachel didn't have a problem with that, but she found herself wondering what her role in Maura's life would be if she and Andrew ever took their relationship to the next level. Blended families were almost the norm now, but that didn't mean they weren't fraught with difficulties.

She felt fortunate that Andrew's daughter was so accepting and affectionate, but she knew there would eventually be conflicts. It was simply the nature of human relationships.

She didn't anticipate that their first conflict would come the very next weekend—or that it would have such far-reaching repercussions.

When Rachel asked Andrew and Maura if they wanted to join Scott, Trent and herself for a picnic in the park and then a game of mini-golf, his daughter immediately responded with an enthusiastic yes. But when Rachel showed up with her nephews on Saturday, Maura refused to come out of her room.

"I don't want to go mini-putting," Maura decided.

"Yesterday you said you did," Andrew reminded her.

"I changed my mind."

"Well, you can't stay here by yourself."

"You can stay with me, Daddy."

"No, I can't," he told her. "Because I made plans with Rachel and Scott and Trent."

Her little brow furrowed. "But you're my daddy. You have to be with me."

"I made a commitment to Rachel," he reminded her. "So if you don't want to come, I'll call Auntie Jordyn to see if she's available to stay with you."

Technically, Jordyn was Maura's second cousin not her aunt, but when Maura was little, she couldn't understand why Nathan and Daniel were her uncles and Braden, Justin and Ryan were her cousins. So she started calling them *uncle* and, by extension, his female cousins, Jordyn, Tristyn and Lauryn, became her aunts.

And although Maura was usually happy to spend time with any one of her aunts or uncles, she crossed her arms over her chest now. "I don't want Auntie Jordyn. I want you."

"Well, I'm going for a picnic."

"With *her*."

Andrew had never heard such venom in his daughter's tone and was taken aback by it now, especially considering that it was directed toward Rachel, whom she completely adored. "If you mean Rachel, then yes."

His daughter's blue eyes filled with tears. "You'd rather be with her than with me."

"I'd rather spend the day with both of you, but you decided that you don't want to go," he said with deliberate patience.

"I don't wanna go," she confirmed.

He left her pouting in her room and went to explain the situation—as best he could because he really didn't understand what had caused her to change her mind—to Rachel.

She immediately offered to take the boys on her own, but he shook his head.

"We made plans," he reminded her. "And I'm not going to renege on them just because my daughter's having a temper tantrum."

But Rachel suspected it might be something more than that. "Can I talk to her?"

"You can try."

While he went to call his cousin, Rachel went up to Maura's room. She knocked lightly on the partially closed door.

"Go away."

"I just want to talk to you, Maura."

"I don't wanna talk to you."

Through the narrow opening, she could see the little girl standing with her back to the door, her arms folded across her chest. Her instincts urged her to push open the door and go into the room, but she held back. Instead, she asked gently, "Did I do something to upset you?"

Maura didn't answer.

"Because if I did, I'm sorry."

The child remained silent.

Rachel sighed. "I wish I knew what to do to make this better, but I can't help if you don't tell me what's wrong."

Finally she turned to face the door. Behind the tears, the little girl's big blue eyes were filled with confusion and sadness, and Rachel wanted only to take her in her arms and offer comfort.

But when Maura spoke, the coldness of her tone assured Rachel that she meant what she said, and she knew that anything she offered would be rejected. "I don't want you to help—I want you to go away."

"If that's really what you want, I will."

Maura's lower lip trembled and fat tears spilled over, tracking slowly down her cheeks. "It's really what I want."

So Rachel nodded and headed back down the stairs.

"Any luck?" Andrew asked.

"No," she admitted.

He exhaled a weary sigh. "Okay. Jordyn's on her way— she should be here in about fifteen minutes." He looked over at the boys, who were on the couch in the living room playing video games while they waited. "I'm really sorry about this—the boys are probably starving."

"They don't seem to be complaining," she noted. "But I do think it's best if we get going and just spend the day by ourselves."

He frowned. "Why?"

"Because I don't want Maura to feel like you're choosing to be with me instead of her."

"Don't you think that's a little melodramatic?"

She shook her head. "No, I don't."

"Whatever's going on with my daughter, she'll get over it," he assured her.

"How can you be sure of that?"

"Because she's seven years old and occasionally moody."

"I don't think this was a simple matter of Maura changing her mind," Rachel noted. "It wasn't about mini-golf so much as spending time with me."

"She loves being with you."

Rachel used to think so. But she'd noticed a distinct change in Maura's attitude toward her since the little girl had come back from her trip to Myrtle Beach. And she didn't think that was a coincidence. She might not know what or how, but she didn't doubt that Carol Wakefield had said or done something to make the child wary of Rachel.

But all she said to Andrew was "Not today she doesn't."

"I'm not going to be forced to make a choice between you and my daughter."

"Of course not," she agreed.

Because she knew that there was no choice to be made—and no hope for a future for them together so long as Maura remained opposed to their relationship.

Rachel dropped the boys off at her brother's house at the usual time, then she went home and poked around in the mostly empty refrigerator to figure out her own dinner before deciding that she wasn't really hungry, anyway. Instead, she curled up on the couch with the television remote in her hand and flipped through various channels, but nothing piqued her interest.

Her heart was breaking, because she knew her relationship with Andrew was over. It had to be over. She couldn't endure another scene like the one that had played out with Maura when she'd refused to go on the picnic.

She still didn't understand what had happened with the

little girl, but she knew it was more than a simple temper tantrum. For some reason, Maura had decided that she didn't want Rachel to be part of her life anymore. And the reason didn't really matter. What mattered was that Rachel couldn't let Andrew get caught in the middle and she couldn't bear to hurt his daughter, who had already been through so much.

Maura was the only part of his wife that he had left, and he was the only parent his child had left. Rachel couldn't blame her for resenting anyone who seemed to threaten that relationship. But she wished the little girl had talked to her, given Rachel a chance to explain that she wasn't trying to come between Andrew and Maura, she only wanted to be part of the family unit that they already were.

Sunday was Mother's Day and, aside from the fact that Andrew and Maura would be visiting his parents and his former in-laws, it was a busy day at Buds & Blooms. Rachel focused on her customers and tried not to think about how much she wanted to be with the sexy single dad and his little girl. On Monday, she and Holly worked steadily to fulfill an order for fifty floral arrangements for a fiftieth birthday party. By the time she got home that night, her fingers were raw and bleeding. And when Andrew called, she didn't have the energy to tackle the discussion she knew they needed to have, so she pretended that everything was okay, cutting their conversation short with the explanation that she was exhausted.

But on Tuesday, she knew she couldn't put it off any longer. She called him this time and asked him to meet her for coffee. It wasn't until she reached for the handle of the door of the Bean There Café that she realized the last time she was here with Andrew was when he'd suggested cooling down their relationship. She wondered if it was apropos that they'd returned to the same place to say goodbye again.

He was already seated with two mugs of coffee on the table when she walked in. He smiled, so genuinely happy to see her that her heart felt as if it would split right open.

She couldn't smile back. She sat down and set his key on the table. He frowned at it. "What's going on, Rachel?"

"I'm sorry…" Her throat was so tight she could barely get the words out. But she had to do this—and she had to get through it without breaking down so that he didn't figure out that everything she was saying was a complete lie. "But I don't want to do this anymore."

He just stared at her, uncomprehending. "Where is this coming from? Why now?"

"Because I realized that we're at different stages in our lives—we want different things." She tried to keep her tone matter-of-fact, so he wouldn't guess that her heart was breaking. "I enjoyed spending time with you and Maura, but I'm not ready to take on the responsibility of some-one else's child."

His gaze narrowed.

"I didn't mean to mislead you—"

"Mislead?" he said incredulously. "I told you I was in love with you, and I thought you were heading in the same direction."

She shook her head, because she wasn't headed in that direction—she'd gone down that road way before him. But admitting that now would only make things harder for both of them. Their feelings for one another didn't—couldn't—matter, not when there was a little girl who was scared and hurting and needed to know that her daddy would always be there for her. And if she told Andrew the truth, that she was stepping back because Maura wasn't as ready for a new family as he thought, she knew that he would try to change her mind. He'd argue that Maura just needed more time, and more time with Andrew and his little girl would only make it that much harder when she finally had to say goodbye. So instead all she said was "I'm sorry."

And then, before he could respond, she pushed back her chair and rushed out of the café.

When she got back to the shop, Holly took one look at her and said, "Spill."

The obvious concern in her friend's eyes was Rachel's undoing. She'd made a valiant effort to hold back her emotions all morning, but now the tears spilled over.

"Oh, Rach. I'm sorry."

She plucked a tissue out of the box on the counter. "Why are you sorry?"

"Because I hate to see you cry."

"I hate to cry," Rachel admitted. "I hate knowing that I made the same mistake and let my heart get broken again."

"Oh." Holly's eyes misted. "You broke up with Andrew."

She nodded.

"Damn." Her friend grabbed a tissue and dabbed at her own eyes. "I really thought he was the one. The guy certainly acted like he was head over heels for you."

"He told me he loved me," Rachel admitted.

Holly's jaw dropped. "And then he dumped you?"

"No." She swiped at more tears. "It was my decision to end things."

"But why? You're obviously as head over heels as he is."

"Because me being with Andrew was making Maura miserable."

"You broke up with him because his seven-year-old was a little miffed about having to share time with her daddy?"

"There was no way we could make a relationship work when his daughter was so obviously unhappy about it."

"She's had him to herself for the past three years—it's natural that there would be some resistance."

"Resistance I could deal with," Rachel agreed. "Maura is downright hostile."

Holly frowned. "What happened?"

She just shook her head, because she didn't know for sure, and she didn't feel comfortable sharing her suspicions about Maura's grandmother with Holly.

Besides, the reason wasn't nearly as important as the result.

Maura was sitting in a chair in the principal's office.

Mrs. Barnhart wasn't there, so she didn't think she was in trouble. And she didn't know why she'd be in trouble when she hadn't done anything wrong, except that she'd started crying in class. Lotsa kids cried in kindergarten, but maybe when you got to first grade, crying got you sent to the principal's office.

Now she was just sitting and waiting for her daddy to show up because Mrs. Patterson was "concerned" about her outburst.

Maura didn't want to talk about it. She didn't understand why the teacher cared that she didn't want to be in the stupid play. It was only for their class anyway, and a lot of the other girls had put up their hands because they wanted what Mrs. Patterson called "the starring role."

Maura looked up when her daddy walked into the room and, for some reason, just seeing him started her crying again.

"What's this about?" he asked Mrs. Patterson.

The teacher shook her head. "I'm as baffled as you are."

He crouched down by her chair. "Maura?"

"I d-don't wanna be in the p-play."

He brushed her hair away from her face and wiped the tears on her cheeks. "Is that what has you so upset?"

She nodded.

He looked at Mrs. Patterson. "Is this a curriculum requirement?"

"Yes, it's part of the drama component, and every student is expected to participate."

He lifted Maura's chin up, forcing her to look at him. "Why don't you want to be in the play?"

"I don't wanna be Cinderella," she said, and burst into tears again.

Andrew went directly to his former in-laws' house after he dropped Maura off at home with Sharlene. He found Carol on the back deck, watering planters filled with flowers. Of course, the sight of those cheerful blooms made him think of Rachel, and the pain that sliced through his chest was so sharp and swift it nearly staggered him.

His former mother-in-law looked up when he stepped onto the deck. She was obviously surprised by his unannounced visit, but she smiled. "Hello, Andrew." She looked past him, hoping to see the little girl who was never far behind. "Where's Maura?"

"She's at home with Sharlene. I didn't want her to overhear any part of the conversation we're going to have."

"Oh?"

"Is Ed around?"

"Right here," Carol's husband said, stepping out onto the deck. "What's going on?"

"I need to talk to both of you."

"What's the matter?" Carol's face went white. "Did something happen to Maura?"

"Maura's fine," he hastened to assure them. "Although she's a very unhappy little girl right now."

"Maybe we should go inside and sit down," Ed suggested.

Andrew nodded and followed him into the house.

"Can I get you anything?" Carol asked. "Coffee? Beer?"

He shook his head. This wasn't a social visit, and he didn't want to give either of them the impression that it was.

"So tell us what this is about," his former father-in-law said, when they were all seated in the living room.

"I want to clear some things up, and then I'm not going to talk about them again," Andrew said.

"Okay," Ed agreed cautiously. His wife nodded.

"I want to start by reminding you that I loved your daughter," he told them sincerely. "Every minute of every day of our life together. I loved her so much that I was sure there wasn't room in my heart for anyone else.

"Then Maura was born, and I realized that the human heart has an infinite capacity for love. There isn't anything I wouldn't have done for either of them." He had to swallow around the lump in his throat. "If there had been any way to save Nina, I would have done so. I would have given my life for hers if I could have."

Carol's eyes filled with tears. Her husband took her hand, linked their fingers together.

"I grieved for a long time," Andrew continued. "I'm not sure I would have got through the darkest days without Maura. She was my reason for getting up in the morning, for moving forward when I wanted to stand still.

"And then—" He swallowed again. "And then I met Rachel."

"Maura said that you aren't seeing her anymore," Carol said, just a little smugly.

He ignored the emptiness in his heart that was an actual physical ache. He wasn't here to talk about Rachel, except insofar as his relationship with her had affected Maura. "The status of my relationship with Rachel—or anyone else—shouldn't be any of your concern."

"I'm concerned about anything that affects my granddaughter," she insisted.

"Your concern crossed the line," Andrew told her.

"I don't know what you mean," she insisted.

But he wasn't buying her innocent act, and the more he thought about what she'd done—using her own granddaughter as a pawn—the angrier he got. "Maura loved spending time with Rachel...until the weekend she spent with you in Myrtle Beach."

"Just what are you implying?" Ed demanded.

"I'm not implying anything. I'm telling both of you that I won't tolerate any more interference in my personal life."

The older man scowled. "I don't know what you're talking about. Maura had a wonderful time at the beach."

Andrew focused on Carol. "Tell him—" He had to clear his throat. "Tell him about the bedtime stories you chose to read to my daughter."

"They were classic fairy tales," she said defiantly.

"Coincidentally the ones that included evil stepmothers."

"That's ridiculous," Ed blustered.

But Carol remained silent.

"She had a meltdown at school today," Andrew told them, his own eyes blurring as he recalled the heart-wrenching sobs that had emanated from his little girl. "Because the class is doing a production of *The Fairy Godmother* and her teacher asked Maura to play Cinderella."

His former mother-in-law pressed a hand to her lips and her eyes filled with tears, but Andrew didn't let himself feel any sympathy for her. It was Maura who mattered—Maura whose innocent heart had been manipulated by her vindictive grandmother.

"Is she okay?" Ed asked.

"She will be," Andrew promised. "But right now, she's scared and hurt and confused. She doesn't know how to feel or what to believe."

A single tear slid down Carol's pale cheek. "They were just stories," she said again.

"I've done everything I can to ensure that Maura has a close bond with both of you," he reminded them. "But I promise you, if you *ever* interfere in my personal life again, I will limit her contact with you."

She gasped. "You wouldn't do that."

"I will if you push me, Carol," he promised.

Then he walked out, confident that he'd made his point to Maura's grandparents. He knew it was going to take a little more work to reassure his daughter, but he would do it.

As for the rest of his life, he didn't have a clue.

Chapter Fifteen

Buds & Blooms wasn't even open yet when JJ called Monday morning to ask Rachel if she could squeeze in a consult around 10:00 a.m. Because she always enjoyed working with the event planner who was also a good friend, she immediately said yes. She didn't know who the client was until Daniel Garrett walked through the door.

Her ready smile froze on her lips; Daniel looked equally startled to see her.

"If this is awkward for you, I can go somewhere else," he said.

"If you need flowers, I'm happy to help," Rachel assured him. At the same time, she reminded herself that she wasn't in the habit of turning away business.

However Daniel had found JJ, it wasn't surprising that her friend had recommended Buds & Blooms. It was just a coincidence—and sheer bad luck for Rachel—that his presence made her think about his brother, and that even nine days after she'd last seen him, just thinking about Andrew still made her heart ache.

"We're having a party to celebrate my parents' fortieth wedding anniversary, and since they're going to renew their vows, JJ suggested that you might be able to replicate my mother's wedding bouquet."

She pushed aside her personal feelings and focused on the job. "Do you have pictures of it?"

JJ immediately opened the folio she carried and removed a couple of photographs.

It was a traditional cascade style of white roses, daisies and chrysanthemums. Simple. Elegant. Beautiful. Her gaze shifted from the flowers to the bride holding them. Jane's head was tilted toward her groom, and a forty years younger David Garrett looked so much like his eldest son that Rachel's breath actually hitched.

"Rachel?" JJ prompted gently.

"Yes." She nodded. "I can do this."

"We need centerpieces for the tables, too," JJ continued. "And I thought it would be nice if we could use the same—or similar—types of flowers."

Rachel nodded again as she made her own notes. "How many centerpieces?"

"Ten tables for guests, plus something for the cake table and maybe a couple of baskets for the pedestals that flank the main doors."

She jotted down the information. "When do you want them?"

When the response to her question wasn't immediately forthcoming, she looked up and saw JJ nudge Daniel. Obviously she wanted him to be the one to answer that question.

"Saturday."

"Date?" she prompted.

He cleared his throat. "May twenty-fourth."

She looked up. "*This* Saturday?"

"Yeah."

Her disbelieving gaze shifted to JJ.

"I told him that if you were able to accommodate his last-minute request, there would be a premium added to the bill," her friend said.

"It's five days away," Daniel noted. "I didn't think that was last-minute."

"Last-minute and the start of wedding season," JJ told them. Then to Rachel, "He called me yesterday, and he knows I'm adding twenty-five percent to my usual fee."

Rachel pulled up the calendar on the computer, looked at the orders she already had to fill for the weekend. If it had been anyone else, she would have turned him away without regret or hesitation. But this was Jane and David's celebration, and she wanted to do this for them. It would mean asking Trish and Elaine to put in some extra hours, but she didn't think either of them would mind.

"If you can only do the bouquet, I'll settle for that," Daniel interjected. "The centerpieces aren't as crucial. I can probably just pick up some fresh cut flowers at the grocery store to stick in vases on the tables."

Both JJ and Rachel gasped in horror.

"I didn't think that was such a bad idea," he mumbled.

"I'll do it," Rachel said. "If I have to work through the night on Friday, I'll make sure you have your bouquet and the centerpieces."

"Thanks," he said.

JJ made some notes. "Okay, now we have to go sweet-talk Gabe Beaulieu to try and get a cake."

Because Rachel knew Gabe, whose shop The Sweet Spot was on the next block and whose disposition was anything but sweet, she said, "Good luck with that."

Daniel paused at the door. "Do you want to come?"

"To face the wrath of Gabe? No thanks."

"I meant to the anniversary party," he clarified. "I know my parents would love to see you."

She shook her head. "That would be awkward."

JJ, sensing that they were talking about something outside of planning the celebration, slipped out the door to give them some privacy.

"I know that whatever happened between you and my brother is none of my business," he said. "And I don't usually interfere in things that aren't my business, but Andrew's been miserable since you split up."

The revelation that he was suffering did nothing to lessen her own pain. Even if Andrew wanted to be with her, even if he loved her, it didn't—couldn't—change anything. Not so long as Maura remained opposed to them being together.

"And I don't think you're much happier," Daniel added.

So much for the radiant glow promised by the cosmetics company, she thought wryly, but forced a smile. "If there's nothing else, I have flowers to order."

"There is one more thing."

She kept the smile in place and waited for him to continue.

"Andrew doesn't do anything in half measures. When he falls in love, it's wholly and completely. And he fell in love with you." He held her gaze for a long moment, then shrugged. "Of course, if you don't feel the same way, then his feelings are his problem, aren't they?"

She felt the sting of tears, but she didn't let them fall. "Love isn't always enough."

"I'm hardly an expert on the subject, but my mother—who is about to celebrate her fortieth wedding anniversary," he reminded her with a smile, "always said that love is the only thing that matters."

She was in the shop early Saturday morning when JJ came by to pick up the flowers for David and Jane Garrett's fortieth wedding anniversary. Since Rachel was busy sorting through the morning delivery, Trish helped load the arrangements into the van.

Two hours later, JJ called.

"I forgot the bouquet."

"You *forgot* the bouquet?" Rachel echoed incredulously.

As an event planner, JJ lived and died by her lists—every detail of every event was cross-referenced and programmed into her electronic organizer. There was no way she forgot anything unless it was on purpose.

"I'm sorry," her friend said. "I know it's an inconvenience to ask you to bring it over—"

"Actually, we're not that busy at the moment, so I'll send Trish with it right now," Rachel offered.

"You would, too, wouldn't you?" JJ muttered, confirming that her forgetfulness had been deliberate.

"Or you could come and get it."

"You're right," JJ agreed. "That's a better idea."

Rachel thought she'd outsmarted the event planner until Andrew and Maura showed up at the shop instead of JJ.

She was grateful she was standing behind the lower part of the elevated counter so that he couldn't see her grip the edge for balance when her knees started to quiver.

Maura skipped into the shop, but stopped several feet away, as if suddenly uncertain. "Hi, Rachel."

She managed a smile. "Well, look at you," she said. "Aren't you pretty as a picture?"

"I got a new dress 'cuz it's a special occasion."

"A very special occasion," Rachel agreed.

"Daddy got dressed up, too."

Rachel had noticed—and the sight of Andrew in the dark blue suit with a crisp white shirt and blue-and-gray tie had made her heart pound and her mouth dry.

When he came closer, she could see that there were shadows under his eyes, as if he hadn't been sleeping well. She knew the feeling.

"Your daddy looks very handsome, too," Rachel noted. Then, to Andrew, "I'll get the bouquet."

She went to the back room, where Trish was making boutonnieres, and retrieved the box from the refrigerator. She desperately wanted to take a minute to catch her breath and steel her spine, but that would mean an extra minute that Andrew and Maura would be waiting out front. And more than she wanted that extra minute, she needed him to go—to get out of her life before he saw that her heart was breaking all over again.

She set the box on the counter, and he peered at the flowers through the window in the lid. "It looks just like the pictures," he said, sounding impressed.

"That was the idea."

"My mother's going to love it."

"I hope so."

"I wanna see," Maura demanded, so he picked her up so that she could look at the bouquet.

"You make really pretty flowers," the little girl said to Rachel.

"Thank you."

"Daddy says that what you do is like art."

"I suppose it is," she agreed.

"I'm not very good at art," Maura admitted, when Andrew had lowered her back to the floor. "Daddy says that everyone needs to be good at different things or the world would be a boring place."

Rachel nodded, wondering where the child was going with this conversation. She wanted to point to the clock, to remind them that they had an anniversary party to go to, but neither Andrew nor his daughter seemed to be in a particular hurry.

"But I had to draw a picture for school," the little girl continued. "And I wanted to give it to you."

She didn't know what to expect as she unfolded the paper that Maura offered to her. The first thing she saw on the top was the A minus in red ink, and she felt a surge of pride for the child who'd claimed she wasn't very good at art. And then she looked at the three figures depicted in the drawing, immediately recognizing Maura, Andrew and herself—except that she was sporting a huge belly. "Oh. Wow."

Her initial surprise was quickly supplanted by an unexpected surge of longing, and tears filled her eyes. She'd always thought she would have children someday, but *someday* had always seemed a long time away. Looking at the child's drawing, she realized that was why ending her relationship with Andrew had hurt so much, because she'd thought he was the one she would share that *someday* with.

For the first time in her life, she'd felt ready to tackle all the wonderful and messy stuff that went along with being a mother. And then she'd realized it wouldn't be with him, because Maura didn't want her to be her new mother.

"It's the first time I got a A in art," Maura told her.

"I think you should have got an A plus."

The little girl smiled at that. "Mrs. Patterson told us to draw a picture of what we most wanted, and I wanted you."

Then she looked down at her feet, and Andrew put a supporting hand on her shoulder, wordlessly encouraging her.

"And then I didn't want you," she admitted in a quiet voice.

There were probably all kinds of things that Rachel could have said, numerous responses that would have assured the child she was entitled to her feelings and that she shouldn't regret or be sad about what was in her heart, but she was incapable of forming any words.

"I told you to go away, and when you did, I missed you."

Her throat tightened.

"I really miss you, Rachel."

Rachel's heart wouldn't let her ignore the entreaty in

the little girl's words. "I miss you, too," she admitted, "but sometimes—"

"Sometimes people do the wrong thing for the right reasons," Andrew interjected, pinning her with his gaze so that she knew he was referring to her actions rather than his daughter's.

Obviously at some point over the past couple of weeks he'd figured out the truth—that she'd walked away from him not because she didn't love him but because she did.

But Maura wasn't finished yet. "I understand if you don't like me anymore—"

Rachel could hardly speak through the tears that clogged her throat, but she couldn't bear for the little girl to think such a thing for even another second. "I couldn't ever stop liking you, Maura."

The tears that trickled down the child's cheeks squeezed her heart.

"What about Daddy? Do you still l-like him, too?"

Like didn't begin to describe the plethora of emotions that she felt for Maura's father. She looked at him now and wished she knew what he was thinking, but his steady gaze gave nothing away. He'd made the first move, bringing Maura here today. And his daughter's courage in owning up to what she'd done, and her willingness to admit her feelings, inspired Rachel to do the same.

"Yeah, I still like your daddy." She looked up and met his gaze across the counter. "In fact, I love him with my whole heart."

He shook his head, but she saw the tension in his shoulders relax and a slight smile tugged at the corners of his mouth. "I can't believe that the first time you say those words is with three feet of granite between us."

"The first time I ever saw you, we were standing on opposite sides of this counter," she reminded him.

He took her hand and guided her around the barrier and into his arms.

"Tell her you love her, too, Daddy," Maura urged.

He pulled Rachel into his arms. "I do, you know."

"And then you hafta kiss her," the little girl said.

"Well, if I have to," he said, and lowered his head.

It felt as if it had been months rather than weeks since she'd been in his arms, since he'd kissed her. But now, with the first touch of his mouth to hers, all the heartache of those weeks melted away.

The chime of Andrew's cell phone forced them apart. With obvious reluctance, he released her to look at the screen. "JJ wants to know the status of the bouquet."

"Then you better get it to her," Rachel advised.

"Come with us," Andrew urged.

"I wish I could, but—"

"I just got off the phone with Holly," Trish interjected, poking her head out from the back room. "She's on her way and she said that you are officially banned from these premises for the rest of the weekend."

Rachel smiled happily and took Maura's hand in hers. "In that case, we've got a party to get to."

Epilogue

Two weeks later

Gemma Palermo greeted Rachel, Andrew and Maura with wide-eyed dismay as soon as they walked in to Valentino's. "You don't have a reservation."

"Do we need one?" Andrew asked.

"The entire dining room is booked for a conference group that's coming in."

Maura's face fell. "But I want p'sgetti."

Gemma glanced at her watch and then back into the dining room. She held up a hand. "Just give me a sec," she said, and disappeared.

"Why don't we just go back to your place?" Rachel suggested to Andrew and Maura. "I can make something for us there."

He shook his head. "We wanted to take you out for dinner because you've been working all day."

"It's not a big deal to make a pot of pasta," she assured him.

Before he could respond, Gemma was back. "We found

somewhere to squeeze you in," she said, then led them through the mostly empty dining room, past numerous vacant tables with Reserved signs on them, and into the kitchen.

Rachel smiled when she saw that one of the workstations had been covered with a linen cloth and set with three place settings, a bottle of wine, candles and a gorgeous bouquet of fresh lilies that she immediately recognized as Holly's handiwork. Except for the third plate, it reminded her of the first night she and Andrew had shared dinner.

She ordered her usual, the penne with sausage and peppers, and Andrew requested the same, with Maura voting for spaghetti and meatballs.

While they ate, Rachel found herself thinking about how much her life had changed in the past four months since she'd first shared a meal with Andrew in this kitchen, and how very lucky she was. She wasn't naive enough to think that there wouldn't be other obstacles in their future, but she was confident that she and Andrew would overcome them together.

"Is it time for dessert now, Daddy?" Maura's question interrupted her musing.

Andrew shook his head. "Rachel hasn't finished her pasta yet."

"Actually, I don't think I can eat another bite," she told him, pushing her plate aside.

It was immediately whisked away by one of the staff.

"Dessert?" Maura prompted again, as Gemma returned to the kitchen.

"Yes," Andrew agreed.

"Let's go see what we can find," Gemma suggested to the little girl.

As Maura skipped off with the hostess, Andrew reached across the table and linked his hand with Rachel's. "What were you thinking about?"

"I was just thinking that I might not hate Valentine's Day anymore."

His brows lifted. "Might not?"

She smiled. "I'll keep you posted."

Further discussion of the topic was curtailed by Maura's return. Andrew drew his hand back as his daughter approached the makeshift table slowly, carrying in both hands a plate with a slice of chocolate raspberry cheesecake.

Rachel was surprised by her choice. Maura wasn't much of a cheesecake fan and she'd figured the little girl would want a sundae. She was even more surprised when Andrew's daughter set the plate on the table in front of her.

The top of the cake was decorated with a sprinkle of powdered sugar and a trio of fresh raspberries, but it was the ring leaning against the fruit that made Rachel's breath catch in her throat: a gold band set with a gorgeous blue diamond encircled by smaller white diamonds.

Her gaze shifted from the ring to the man seated across the table.

"Maura picked it out," he explained. "Because it looked like a flower. But if you don't like it—"

"It's beautiful," she assured him, her heart pounding so hard against her ribs she was certain both Andrew and Maura must be able to hear it.

"I wanted to wait for our six-month anniversary, but somebody—" he looked pointedly at his daughter "—was a little impatient."

The little girl just grinned, clearly unchastised. "Ask her, Daddy."

"Give him a chance," Gemma said to the child.

But the excitement and anticipation on her friend's face made Rachel suspect that the Reserved signs all over the dining room had been put there solely for her benefit, that there wasn't any conference group coming into the restaurant for dinner, after all. The whole scene had been deliberately set up to get Rachel into the kitchen where she and Andrew had dined together on Valentine's Day.

"This isn't quite how I planned for this to happen," he admitted to Rachel. "When I first decided that I was going to ask you to marry me, I imagined something a little more intimate, something for just you and me.

"But the reality is, it's not going to be just you and me. Maura and I are a package deal, so it seemed appropriate that instead of asking you to share my life, we should ask you to share our life, to be part of our family, for now and forever."

He reached across the table for her hand again. "What do you think?"

She drew in a deep breath. "I think that, as far as proposals go, yours was almost perfect."

"Almost?"

"You didn't get down on one knee, Daddy," Maura told him.

He slid from his chair to kneel on the kitchen floor beside Rachel's.

And the moment was more perfect than anything she could have imagined. Except for one thing. "Actually, I was thinking more about the part where you forgot to ask the question."

"Right." He smiled sheepishly. "Rachel Ellis, will you marry me?"

Though her heart was so full she could barely speak, she knew that the question asked deserved more than a silent nod. "Yes, Andrew Garrett, I will marry you."

Maura took the ring off the cake and gave it to her father so he could slide it on Rachel's finger. Then the kitchen staff erupted into spontaneous applause as he kissed her.

"When are we gonna have the wedding?" Maura wanted to know.

Andrew chuckled. "We'll figure that out soon enough."

"But yes," Rachel said, before her soon-to-be daughter could ask. "You can be the flower girl."

"Yippee!"

After accepting congratulations from Gemma and Tony and the rest of the staff, Rachel offered one hand to Maura, Andrew took the other and they walked out of Valentino's kitchen together, hand in hand in hand.

Finally, a family.

* * * * *

It was supposed to be a marriage of convenience between two friends...until one kiss changed everything....
Don't miss Daniel & Kenna's story!

Look for
A WIFE FOR ONE YEAR
by award-winning author Brenda Harlen.

The next installment of
THOSE ENGAGING GARRETTS!

On sale August 2014,
wherever Harlequin books are sold.

COMING NEXT MONTH FROM

HARLEQUIN®

SPECIAL EDITION

Available June 19, 2014

#2341 MILLION-DOLLAR MAVERICK

Montana Mavericks: 20 Years in the Saddle! • by Christine Rimmer

Cowboy Nate Crawford epitomizes the phrase "new money." He secretly just won millions in the lottery, and he can't wait to cash out and leave Rust Creek Falls. But then Nate meets gorgeous nurse Callie Kennedy, who doesn't give a flying Stetson about money, and all he's ever dreamed of might be in the home he wants to leave behind....

#2342 DATING FOR TWO

Matchmaking Mamas • by Marie Ferrarella

Erin O'Brien is too busy bringing her toy company to new heights to play house with just any man. But speaking at a local Career Day might lead to a whole new job—mommy! When she meets hunky lawyer Steve Kendall and his son, Erin can't help but fall for the adorable twosome. Will Erin be the missing piece in their family puzzle?

#2343 THE BACHELOR'S BRIGHTON VALLEY BRIDE

Return to Brighton Valley • by Judy Duarte

Clayton Jenkins is going undercover...in his own business. The tech whiz wants to find out why his flagship store is failing, so he disguises himself as an employee and gets to work. But even a genius can't program every step of his life—like falling for single mom Megan Adams and her young children! What's a billionaire to do?

#2344 READY, SET, I DO!

Rx for Love • by Cindy Kirk

Workaholic Winn Ferris receives the surprise of his life when he gets custody of an eight-year-old boy. He enlists neighbor Hailey Randall to help him with the child, but Winn can't help but marvel at the bubbly speech therapist. She might just be the one to lift the businessman's nose from the grindstone to gaze into her beautiful baby blues—and fall in love....

#2345 A BRIDE BY SUMMER

Round-the-Clock Brides • by Sandra Steffen

Apple orchard owner Reed Sullivan is frantic with worry when a baby appears on his doorstep. Did his one-night stand from a year ago yield a (too) fruitful crop? So Reid's blindsided when a radiant redhead rescues him from a car accident. Ruby O'Toole has sworn off men, but the quirky bar owner might have it bad for the man she saved—and his insta-family!

#2346 A DOCTOR FOR KEEPS

by Lynne Marshall

Desdemona "Desi" Rask shows up on her grandmother's doorstep to learn about her family in the town of Heartlandia. But Fate throws a wrench in her plans when she meets Dr. Kent Larson and his adorable son. As Desi discovers more about her relatives, she wonders: Can she have a future with Kent, or will her past keep them apart forever?

HSECNM0614

REQUEST YOUR FREE BOOKS!
2 FREE NOVELS PLUS 2 FREE GIFTS!

⊞ HARLEQUIN®

SPECIAL EDITION
Life, Love & Family

YES! Please send me 2 FREE Harlequin® Special Edition novels and my 2 FREE gifts (gifts are worth about $10). After receiving them, if I don't wish to receive any more books, I can return the shipping statement marked "cancel." If I don't cancel, I will receive 6 brand-new novels every month and be billed just $4.74 per book in the U.S. or $5.24 per book in Canada. That's a savings of at least 14% off the cover price! It's quite a bargain! Shipping and handling is just 50¢ per book in the U.S. and 75¢ per book in Canada.* I understand that accepting the 2 free books and gifts places me under no obligation to buy anything. I can always return a shipment and cancel at any time. Even if I never buy another book, the two free books and gifts are mine to keep forever.

235/335 HDN F45Y

Name _____ (PLEASE PRINT)

Address _____ Apt. #

City _____ State/Prov. _____ Zip/Postal Code

Signature (if under 18, a parent or guardian must sign) _____

Mail to the Harlequin® Reader Service:
IN U.S.A.: P.O. Box 1867, Buffalo, NY 14240-1867
IN CANADA: P.O. Box 609, Fort Erie, Ontario L2A 5X3

Want to try two free books from another line?
Call 1-800-873-8635 or visit www.ReaderService.com.

* Terms and prices subject to change without notice. Prices do not include applicable taxes. Sales tax applicable in N.Y. Canadian residents will be charged applicable taxes. Offer not valid in Quebec. This offer is limited to one order per household. Not valid for current subscribers to Harlequin Special Edition books. All orders subject to credit approval. Credit or debit balances in a customer's account(s) may be offset by any other outstanding balance owed by or to the customer. Please allow 4 to 6 weeks for delivery. Offer available while quantities last.

Your Privacy—The Harlequin® Reader Service is committed to protecting your privacy. Our Privacy Policy is available online at www.ReaderService.com or upon request from the Harlequin Reader Service.

We make a portion of our mailing list available to reputable third parties that offer products we believe may interest you. If you prefer that we not exchange your name with third parties, or if you wish to clarify or modify your communication preferences, please visit us at www.ReaderService.com/consumerschoice or write to us at Harlequin Reader Service Preference Service, P.O. Box 9062, Buffalo, NY 14269. Include your complete name and address.

HSE13R

Enjoy this sneak preview of
DATING FOR TWO
by USA TODAY bestselling author Marie Ferrarella!

***

"Well, you'll be keeping your word to them—I'll be the one doing the cooking."

One of the things he'd picked up on during his brief venture into the dating realm was that most professional women had no time—or desire—to learn how to cook. He'd just naturally assumed that Erin was like the rest in that respect.

"Didn't you say that you were too busy trying to catch up on everything you'd missed out on doing because you were in the hospital?"

"Yes, and cooking was one of those things." She laughed. "A creative person has to have more than one outlet in order to feel fulfilled and on top of their game. Me, I come up with some of my best ideas cooking. Cooking relaxes me," she explained.

"Funny, it has just the opposite effect on me," he said.

"Your strengths obviously lie in other directions," she countered.

Steve had to admit he appreciated the way she tried to spare his ego.

He watched Erin as she practically whirled through his kitchen, getting unlikely ingredients out of his pantry and his cupboard. She assembled everything on the counter within easy reach, then really got busy as she began making dinner.

He had never been one who enjoyed being kept in the dark. "If you don't mind my asking, exactly what do you plan on making?"

"A frittata," she said cheerfully. Combining a total of eight eggs in a large bowl, she tossed in a dash of salt and pepper before going on to add two packages of the frozen mixed vegetables. She would have preferred to use fresh vegetables, but beggars couldn't afford to be choosers.

"A what?"

In another pan, she'd quickly diced up some of the ham she'd found as well as a few slices of cheddar cheese from the same lower bin drawer in the refrigerator.

She was about to repeat the word, then realized that it wasn't that Steve hadn't heard her—the problem was that he didn't know what she was referring to.

Opening the pantry again, she searched for a container of herbs or spices. There were none. She pushed on anyway, adding everything into the bowl with the eggs.

"Just think of it as an upgraded omelet. You have ham and bread," she said, pleased.

"That's because I also know how to make a sandwich without setting off the smoke alarm," he told her.

"There is hope for you yet," she declared with a laugh.

Watching her move around his kitchen as if she belonged there, he was beginning to think the same thing himself—but for a very different reason.

***

Don't miss DATING FOR TWO,
coming July 2014 from Harlequin® Special Edition.

Copyright © 2014 by Marie Rydzynski-Ferrarella

Love the Harlequin book you just read?

Your opinion matters.

Review this book on your favorite book site, review site, blog or your own social media properties and share your opinion with other readers!

Be sure to connect with us at:
Harlequin.com/Newsletters
Facebook.com/HarlequinBooks
Twitter.com/HarlequinBooks